LEIGH DOVEY

The Fallow Field

Leigh Dovey

Published by Leigh Dovey, 2024.

This is a work of fiction. Similarities to real people, places, or events are entirely coincidental.

THE FALLOW FIELD

First edition. May 7, 2024.

Copyright © 2024 Leigh Dovey.

ISBN: 979-8223972266

Written by Leigh Dovey.

Table of Contents

Title Page 1
Copyright Page 2
The Fallow Field 6
CHAPTER ONE 9
CHAPTER TWO 12
CHAPTER THREE 16
CHAPTER FOUR 20
CHAPTER FIVE 23
CHAPTER SIX 27
CHAPTER SEVEN 31
CHAPTER EIGHT 37
CHAPTER NINE 42
CHAPTER TEN 48
CHAPTER ELEVEN 54
CHAPTER TWELVE 59
CHAPTER THIRTEEN 63
CHAPTER FOURTEEN 69
CHAPTER FIFTEEN 73
CHAPTER SIXTEEN 78
CHAPTER SEVENTEEN 84
CHAPTER EIGHTEEN 90
CHAPTER NINETEEN 95
CHAPTER TWENTY 98
CHAPTER TWENTY-ONE 104
CHAPTER TWENTY-TWO 113
CHAPTER TWENTY-THREE 116
CHAPTER TWENTY-FOUR 120
CHAPTER TWENTY-FIVE 126
CHAPTER TWENTY-SIX 128
CHAPTER TWENTY-SEVEN 139

English Soil
An Introduction to The Fallow Field
by
Andrew David Barker

I first met Leigh Dovey on the French Riviera. Far from English soil. It was 2008 and I was at the Cannes Film Festival for the first time, and I was as green as can be. My friend and occasional co-writer, Matthew Waldram, were out there hawking a couple of our screenplays, taking meetings, schmoozing, talking to producers, without having the slightest idea of what we were doing. We were starry-eyed, from seeing the likes of George Lucas and Steven Spielberg and Woody Allen on the Red Carpet, to having Harvey Weinstein barrel down a corridor straight towards, screaming at the two lickspittles by his side, to standing alone in the lobby of the Hotel Le Majestic with Faye Dunaway (I was too frightened to speak to her). Matt and I were running up and down the Croisette like a couple of idiots (not to mention drinking far too much of the free bar at the Scandinavian Film Council every day at 4 pm). Then, one night, a little inebriated, we drifted into a crowd hanging out in the courtyard of the massive Carlton Hotel. There were two guys. One short, one tall. The short one was the talker, the player, the one holding court. This was a producer named Colin Arnold. The other guy, the taller, quieter of the two, was some dude named Leigh Dovey. It turned out they were out in Cannes raising money to shoot their first feature: a low-budget horror entitled The Fallow Field. Leigh was to write and direct it. I was very impressed. These guys were doing it!

Me and Leigh seemed to click right away. It was just one of those times in life when you meet someone and immediately feel at ease. We had the same reference points (an important thing for men), a shared unease and distrust of the film industry (a constant push/pull within us), and a similar mindset when it came to our ambitions and our creativity. After the festival, Leigh and I kept in touch. He would keep me in the loop on the production of The Fallow Field and it inspired and spurred me on to begin work on my own debut feature, A Reckoning. Leigh shot his film in the summer of 2008, and I shot mine in the winter of 2009. What's interesting to me now (and a little sad, I must say) is that we pretty much made these films together, encouraging each other onwards, and yet, neither of us made another feature. To date, anyway. Leigh got his film picked up and released (I didn't), and I remember being so excited when I got a copy of the DVD. I even got Leigh to sign it. He did it and the film was dark and thoughtful and tapped into something that has always interested me: the eeriness of the English landscape.

The Fallow Field shares its lineage with a series of British horror films from the 1970s: mainly gritty thrillers and occult horrors, as well as the famed unholy trilogy of Witchfinder General (Michael Reeves, 1968), Blood on Satan's Claw (Piers Haggard, 1971) and The Wicker Man, (Robin Hardy, 1973). Of these films, The Fallow Field shares the closest lineage to Satan's Claw. The idea of something buried in the English soil, unearthed to contaminate the countryside with its evilness. Folk horror is not exclusive to British cinema, but these three pioneering films certainly set the templates for the subgenre: that of horror coming from the land, the rural settings, the superstitions and sacrifices, the rituals and rites of ancient religions, and the darker elements of nature. All of this features in Dovey's film and the subsequent novelisation, which you now hold in your hands.

The Fallow Field is an intimate horror story, essentially a two-hander between the amnesiac Matt Sadler and farmer Calham, one dangerous individual. The film was produced on a minuscule budget, but what Dovey and his production team achieved on such constraints is impressive, but the novel broadens the narrative - it digs deeper, if you'll forgive the pun - to produce a richly detailed character study of a man coming to realise the true nature of the reoccurring nightmare he is in. The endless loop of horror.

The English landscape plays a major role in both the film and book, and you can feel Dovey's understanding of the ancient eeriness of this Isle. The blood that has seeped into the earth over the centuries, the old myths, the Pagan Gods, the hauntology of a country defined by its strange customs and ancient rites. The old ways. All of this is layered into Dovey's writing.

The Fallow Field is pitch black folk horror. The English soil brims with evil. Turn the page and see...

Andrew David Barker
Warwickshire, April 2024

CHAPTER ONE

A shroud of early morning mist lay deep in the pockets between a horizon of empty, green hills and clung to the agricultural lowlands beyond. A lone black speck marked the centre of one of the many sloping fields at the foot of the hills. It was the crunched form an unconscious man in the wet grass, curled tightly into a foetal ball against the drizzling rain. Matt Sadler suddenly spasmed and woke. He automatically unfurled and sat bolt upright, desperately sucking in an urgent lungful of cold morning air. His breathing then flattened and regulated, and his panic subsided. He slowly looked around, bluntly taking in the surrounding countryside through dazed eyes, without any recognition or understanding. He instinctively rubbed at his aching arms and then at the dull pain swelling at the base of his neck.

The tired-looking thirty-something stood up unsteadily, his muscles and balance adjusting to the task of supporting his upright weight. He slowly rotated through three-hundred and sixty-degrees, surveying the empty landscape around him.

Just the start of another gray day in the British countryside.

Except Matt had no recollection of this area, or how he'd come to be here.

He instinctively reached into the back pocket of his jeans and retrieved a wallet. He quickly opened it and checked inside. A healthy wad of ten and twenty-pound notes were stuffed into the leather, so evidently he hadn't been robbed. Matt slipped out his driving license and examined it. A photo of his younger self gazed back at him, though he didn't recognise the man in the photograph either. He let his hands drop to his sides and stared out across the bleak horizon again, unable to remember a Goddamn thing.

The chilly, moist morning air found its way deeper into Matt's muscles and the resulting ache nagged him out of his daze. His haunted, confused eyes scanned the horizon again, and this time picked out a distant road. He took a deep breath and began to pick his way through the damp grass towards it.

Matt eventually worked his way across the uneven terrain to the road and climbed over a cattle fence to reach it. He then paused, and stood there for a moment in the country lane, looking up and down it, unsure which way to go. Neither memory nor inspiration intervened, so he took potluck and began trudging along in the direction he was already facing. He forlornly followed the lane with shuffling steps, wondering how far he'd have to walk to reach civilisation. Soon the drizzle thickened to full on rain, leaving Matt soaked through in just his T-shirt and jeans. He hugged himself as he walked, trying in vain to keep warm.

It was nearly an hour later when he finally heard a car engine and looked around to see a Toyota approaching from behind. He tried to flag it down, but the car passed him by. Then, moments later its brake lights flared red, and it slowed to a halt just ahead of him. Matt jogged towards the car and climbed in. The Toyota pulled away as the rain became a downpour.

* * *

The Toyota turned into a street of crammed, but well-maintained terraced houses and crawled to a stop. Matt climbed out of the car and waved a thank-you to the driver. He then turned and took the final few steps home, or at least to the address listed on his driving license. He glanced up at *his house* before rummaging in his pockets and fishing out a set of keys. He stood on the front step examining one unfamiliar key after another, looking bemused.

Sandra opened the front door to her dishevelled husband. She looked the worse for wear too and obviously hadn't slept for some time.

Not since Matt had gone missing.

At least he recognised her though, even if all the memories associated with the person were slow to manifest and fully connect to his current self. He smiled at her. She in turn, stared through him without emotion.

Matt heard a car horn behind him. He turned back briefly and raised his hand again to wave at the Good Samaritan behind the wheel as they pulled away. When he turned back to face Sandra the doorway was empty.

CHAPTER TWO

Matt descended the stairs in fresh, dry clothes, idly rubbing at his wet hair with a towel. He was greeted by the sounds of Sandra slamming cups and cupboard doors in the kitchen, channeling her anger into tea making. Matt took the hint and avoided the kitchen, choosing the lounge sofa instead. He limply watched Sandra sweep in and bang down a steaming mug on the coffee table in front of him. She returned to the kitchen without a word, continuing to express her anger through her domestic percussion instead.

Matt reached for the mug, but his hand spasmed uncontrollably. His fingers trembled and then automatically spread themselves to disperse the sensation. He clenched his fist and released it again, rubbing his hand and then his forearm, chasing the pulsing ache away.

The doorbell rang. Matt waited until it became obvious that Sandra had no intention of opening the front door. He trudged along the hallway and opened the door to reveal a stern-looking middle-aged man in a suit. The man looked at him questioningly.

"Matthew Sadler?"

Matt nodded.

The man produced a black wallet and opened it to reveal a police badge.

"Do you mind if I ask you a few questions?"

*　*　*

The police officer took a seat across from Matt and opened up a notebook. He noticed Sandra taking the chair adjacent to him, even though there was ample room on the couch next to Matt.

"You were reported missing a week ago, Mr. Sadler," said the policeman. "Can you tell me where you've been for the last seven days?"

"No," said Matt.

"You don't remember?"

"No," said Matt again.

"You don't remember anything?"

"No, not a thing."

The policeman sighed and looked at Sandra before closing his notebook.

"This isn't the first time this has happened, is it, Mr. Sadler?"

Matt looked across at Sandra too, but she just stared directly ahead without acknowledging him.

"Apparently not," said Matt.

"Well, I'm no doctor," said the policeman. "But I think you better get yourself down to your GP for an examination. A thorough examination."

Matt gazed at them both, as if not really comprehending.

"Is that clear, Mr. Sadler?"

"Yeah," said Matt. "Yeah. I'll do that."

The police officer huffed and rose wearily from his chair.

"Well, if there's nothing else," he said. "I'll go and tie up the paperwork..."

"Actually, there is," said Matt. "I'd like to report my car as stolen."

The police officer rolled his eyes and let out another sigh of resignation. He slumped back down and flipped open his notebook again.

Sandra had finally had enough too. She abruptly stood up and left, her thumping footsteps tracking up the stairs and across the ceiling to the bedroom.

* * *

Matt watched silently from the bed as Sandra took a sheet and blanket out of the closet and snatched up her pillow from her side of the bed. She bundled the improvised bedding into her arms and left without looking at him, shutting the bedroom door behind her.

Matt closed his eyes and tried to rub away the recurring ache that had returned in the back of his neck and migrated to his head again.

* * *

It was pitch black.

Somewhere a baby was screaming.

There was motion within the blackness, but it wasn't clear or properly defined. Sharp, desperate movement, but without detail.

The baby's screams began to grow louder.

The movements in the dark loosened what appeared to be earth, and soil finally crumbled away and tumbled towards him.

He was underground.

Claustrophobic.

Buried deep and desperately tunneling for the surface, he struggled against the crushing weight above him. For every handful of black earth he scraped away, twice as much was released to take its place.

The infant's screaming became even louder, competing with his own rasping, hurried breaths of rising panic, as he scrabbled at the falling earth, clawing it away in vain.

* * *

Matt's desperate, fearful eyes snapped open in the here and now and he escaped the nightmare. He quickly wriggled free from the confines of his twisted duvet and stood up, naked in the middle of the darkened bedroom, relishing the chance to re-establish his own space. He then moved to the window and drew back the curtains, embracing the cold light and relief that came flooding into the room to chase away his claustrophobia.

CHAPTER THREE

Matt wandered into the kitchen in just his boxers, to find Sandra almost ready for the office. In sharp contrast to her recent haggard appearance from the late nights of worry and fear, she now looked smart and attractive; all business. Her features were icy, resolved. She had finally decided to release any lingering concern for Matt and wanted him to see this. She ignored him, sipping her coffee with her back to him and then rummaging around in her handbag without looking up. Matt watched her, waiting for an opportunity to speak, feeling her gradually slide further away from him. The tension in the air slowly thickened.

Finally, Sandra turned to face Matt and made straight for the door. Matt instinctively blocked the doorway, forcing her to at least acknowledge him.

"It's Sunday," he said. "How come you're going in?"

Sandra glanced over his shoulder at her escape route through the hallway and fiddled anxiously with her earring.

"I get it," said Matt. "You're really, really mad at me. I get it."

Sandra made eye contact, but just stared at him coldly before finally speaking.

"Yesterday was mad," she said. "And the days before that."

"So today?" said Matt.

Sandra just shrugged her shoulders nonchalantly. "I've decided to let it go. I don't need this."

"I swear to you, love," said Matt. "I can't remember anything."

"It doesn't matter, Matt. Just do us both a favour. Take your next little walkabout today. I want you out of here when I get back. Whoever she is, she's welcome to you."

Sandra maintained a perfect dead stare as Matt searched her eyes for a glimmer of hope or connection; but there was none. Her icy gaze just bored the message right through him, until he finally relented and stood aside. She walked away without so much as a pause. His dark eyes followed her out of their home and out of his life.

"I love you..." he said, as she slammed the front door, cutting him dead.

* * *

Matt sat on the sofa smoking cigarette after cigarette, lost somewhere in his empty thoughts. After a while something occurred to him, and he jumped up and began rifling through the contents of his bookcase. He took a road atlas from one of the shelves and looked up Shropshire and Herefordshire. He unfolded the pull-out map within and spread it out across the coffee table and began to study it. He lit another cigarette and carefully traced his fingers across the map, trying to establish some route, but the process seemed to leave him even more confused. He finished the cigarette and stared into space again.

All the time wondering where the hell he'd been.

Matt reached for the house phone, but then thought better of it and picked up his mobile instead. He recalled "Ann" from his contacts list and rang.

"It's me," he said. "No, I need to see you...today."

* * *

Matt wandered out of the Hertz office and climbed into a rental on the forecourt. Rain began to fleck against the windows of the Mazda, as he started her up and pulled away. On the way to his lover's house, Matt found himself staring blankly through the rain-splattered windscreen, past the hypnotic nodding of the wiper blades and along the open road ahead. It was if he was travelling some preordained route; more a passenger than a driver.

Matt slowed the Mazda as it approached the sleepy village of Pontrilas. He crawled slowly past Ann's corner cottage, checking around for signs of her boyfriend's car. He craned and looked both ways past his lover's cottage, but it seemed that the coast was clear. Matt pulled over and left the Mazda in the next road down, just in case. On his way up to Ann's cottage, Matt noticed the stern face of an elderly woman peering at him through next door's window. She frowned at him and tracked his progress up to Ann's door.

Ann opened the front door before Matt could knock. The slightly older, attractive brunette let him in quickly without a word.

* * *

In the bedroom, Ann writhed beneath Matt as he pumped away furiously. Both of them climaxed quickly and together, though Matt's finish was so intense it left his head spinning and his eyes fluttering uncontrollably. Matt rolled off and gasped, still twitching. He grabbed a handful of the bed sheet and used it to wipe away a sheen of sweat from his face and chest.

Ann eyed his elated condition with faint surprise and amusement.

"I'm flattered," she said. "Or aren't you getting any at home these days?"

Matt sighed, still coming down from his high. He felt like a kid spinning from the delirious thrill of his first ejaculation. He rolled over and tried to kiss Ann on the lips, just as he'd done a hundred times before after their lovemaking, but this time she resisted.

Ann rose quickly and threw on her robe.

"Two sugars, right?

"Yeah," said Matt. "I take it you're trying to get rid of me."

Ann lingered in the doorway and nodded feebly at him.

"I was hoping we could talk," said Matt.

"Sure," said Ann. "We need to have a chat..."

Ann turned and abruptly disappeared into the hall. Matt sighed again; he already knew what was coming next. He rubbed at his tired eyes. Nothing felt right since the last blackout. It was as if his body was somehow rebelling against him, as if it was no longer his. His right hand suddenly spasmed and began trembling, as if it had heard his thoughts and decided to confirm them. Matt made a fist and purposely held it with some effort until the contractions died away. He continued to stare at his errant hand for a while after, trying to cast dark, half formed thoughts from his mind.

CHAPTER FOUR

Matt stooped as he entered the lounge, finding the cramped confines of the cottage's low-beamed ceiling even more claustrophobic than usual. Ann placed a coffee on the table in front of the couch, hinting that he should sit there, and then strategically took the lone chair opposite him for herself. He immediately noticed that her body language had changed. It was now formal, almost awkward and defensive.

"OK," said Matt. "Spit it out then."

Ann lit herself a cigarette and slid the pack across to him, stalling. He patiently took one out and lit it too, waiting for her inevitable speech.

"I can't do it anymore," she finally said. "Me and Alan are starting to get serious. And this place is...small. They don't miss a trick around here."

"It's not a problem," said Matt. "We can meet up somewhere else."

"No," said Ann. "Thanks all the same, but I think we should call it quits."

Matt sat alone in silence, inhaling the facts and exhaling smoke.

"That's got to be some sort of record," he finally said. "Dumped twice in one day."

"Sorry," said Ann. "Wait, you...you didn't tell her about us, did you?"

"I didn't need to," said Matt. "I had another one of my notorious blackouts and...well I think there was more than enough circumstantial evidence, don't you?"

"You don't look well, Matt," said Ann. "You know, I just don't think you're really built for infidelity. I think maybe your guilt's catching up with you, you know, subconsciously."

Ann examined the lines on Matt's weary face as she exhaled her smoke confidently. Apparently she was relaxing into pop psychology now that she knew he wasn't going to make a scene.

"Maybe you should see someone," she said. "A doctor."

"Maybe," said Matt.

"What are you going to do now?"

"I don't know," said Matt. "It's been a funny old week. Are you really serious about Alan?"

"Does it matter?"

Matt shrugged and took his cue, stubbing out the cigarette in the ashtray. He stood up to leave and Ann rose with him. It looked as if they might move in for one last goodbye kiss, but both of them faltered at the last moment and settled for an awkward excuse for a hug instead. Matt headed towards the door, but stopped and turned back to face her one more time. He had a confused frown on his face.

"What time did I leave here last week?"

"I don't know," said Ann. "About three?"

"Did I say anything before I went? Like where I was going?"

"No," she said. "You just slapped my ass and whispered something in my ear that I'm not about to repeat."

Matt nodded as a faint smile played across his lips.

"*I remember that*," he said. "Take care of yourself, Ann."

* * *

Matt left without looking back. He walked slowly to the car, genuinely trying to remember what had happened to him the week before when he left Ann's. He knew he'd been here, the two of them making love that day was the last fully intact memory still in his head, but what came after it?

Matt stopped on the street corner and rotated, carefully examining his surroundings. There was nothing to see. Just a quiet country village under dark skies spitting rain. He climbed back into the Mazda and started the engine. He sat there for a moment in neutral, looking at the T-junction ahead of him. He then put the car in gear and pulled forwards to the head of the junction. He looked along the road he had come in on, and then across in the opposite direction, through the village centre and out towards the rolling green hills that lay beyond.

"Maybe I took the scenic route." he said to himself.

Matt pulled away and turned right, towards the village and the open countryside on the horizon.

CHAPTER FIVE

Matt's progress through the village was slow. He was forced to crawl behind a horse-drawn cart adorned with bright garlands of flowers trundling along the road, halting traffic. The cart eventually turned off into the driveway of an old church, where it was greeted by grinning parishioners laden with baskets of vegetables and corn dollies. Matt could hear a choir singing harvest time hymns inside the church. 'We Plough the Fields and Scatter' bled out through the church's open arched doors. Matt saw suspicious stares in the faces of locals congregated outside the church as he accelerated away.

After that Matt's journey was free and clear on empty country roads, winding away from the villages and up into the surrounding woods and hills. Not that he knew where he was going. He scanned the countryside carefully, as he cut down one lane after another, letting his instincts guide him, all the while searching for landmarks that might jog his memory and confirm his intuitive route. The Mazda followed one deserted country lane after another, heading deeper and deeper into the middle of a picturesque nowhere. Matt lit a cigarette and let it dangle from his lips, as he surveyed the passing landscape. A derelict, tumbledown windmill appeared before him on the horizon. Matt eyed it carefully and slowed, then stopped the car altogether. The old windmill stirred the vaguest of memories in his head.

"Scenic route," said Matt, pulling away again. A few miles on from the windmill, the Mazda reached a fork in the road. Matt sat at the head of the two roads, his fingers drumming impatiently on the steering wheel as the Mazda's engine idled. He looked back and forth between the two routes on offer for a few moments, before taking the road on the left.

The Mazda weaved back and forth with the heavily twisting lane for a further five miles, picking its way through an increasingly dense and dark wood. Suddenly Matt spun the steering wheel on impulse and guided the Mazda off the road and into the woods along the merest hint of a dirt track. The car shook its way along the track, jolting about violently, forcing Matt to steer the wheel this way and that to compensate for the loose earth beneath its tyres. Then Matt turned sharply again, almost sensing the next junction before he could see it, and pulled the Mazda into a small, remote clearing. He killed the engine.

Matt's eyes grew wide as they stared at something up ahead. He climbed out of the car and slowly approached another vehicle.

It was his own abandoned car.

Matt circled the Montego in a daze. He scanned the empty woods that encircled the clearing, but there was no sign of anyone else present. He finally rummaged in his pockets and pulled out his keys. He tried the Montego's key in the car's door and the driver's side popped open.

Matt climbed in behind the wheel. The seat and mirrors were already adjusted to fit his height and fame. It was a perfect fit.

He examined the dash, drew his fingers across the stereo, and then over a half-eaten packet of nuts next to the gearstick. He felt the tatty, plush dog dangling from the rear-view mirror. Matt slowly soaked up the full realisation that this really was his car, and that he instinctively knew he'd been here before, even though the memory of this place still evaded him.

Matt eased himself out of the Montego and stared at a thin foot trail up ahead. It appeared to lead far away from the clearing, cutting deeper into the woods. Matt locked the Montego's door and headed off down the trail. In no time at all he was consumed by the dense, dark woods surrounding the clearing.

Matt trudged through the woods, constantly looking for clues that might ignite his faded memories. He breathed deeply of the country air, sampling it for any evocative smells. It was all so familiar to him, yet he still couldn't remember having been this way before.

He reached the edge of the woods and found a golden tide of high corn swaying in the breeze beyond the treeline. Matt stood there at the threshold of the field, bemused by the presence and height of such unnaturally tall corn. After a few moments he stepped into the hypnotic, lazy curtain of gold, as it leaned this way and that, gently being manipulated by the autumn winds. Matt disappeared into the corn and began tracking a route between the giant stalks. He carefully made his way through the crop, peering and pushing away the long stalks to clear a path. He finally divided the last of the corn and revealed another clearing up ahead, and within it, Shadowbrook Farm.

The run-down farm was nestled between several other cornfields under a bleak and brooding sky. The tired-looking farmhouse had two large, dilapidated barns set off to one side, but there were no other neighbours in sight. Matt cocked his head as he stared at the scene. Indistinct recollection stirred behind his eyes, but failed to coalesce in his fogged mind. Still, there was something there, something inside, enough to tell him he was on the right track. He pushed on towards the farm and began to hear the low, steady chug of distant generator as he drew nearer.

CHAPTER SIX

Even in the failing light of the late afternoon, Matt could instantly see how neglected the old farm had become. Tractor ploughs and harvesting blades sat idle and rusting next to the rotten wooden sidings of the barns. The only sign that the crumbling farmhouse might still be occupied was an old beat-up Land Rover parked outside.

As Matt approached the farmhouse, a large, sloping fallow field became visible, revealed to him from its hiding place behind the corn and immediately adjacent to the rear of the building. Matt stopped to stare at the vast plot of barren earth, and once again felt memories rise and bubble up in his mind that ultimately failed to surface no matter how hard he tried to force them.

The sound of clinking metal, like links unfurling from a coiled chain, roused Matt from his introspection. He turned to face the source of the noise - the barns. Matt made his way over towards them, hearing the sound again. Now he was sure it was coming from the farthest barn. The sound was different the second time. It was duller, blunter, more like a heavy, slack chain dragging, slowly being pulled taught against a weight. Something made Matt hesitate as he neared the barn's doors. He paused outside, but the pull of curiosity overcame his caution, and he slowly reached out to slide the thick, rusted bolt there free.

Matt jumped as a dog began barking behind him. He turned to see an angry border collie just a few feet away. It was advancing on him, edging closer with each bark.

Something else then caught Matt's eye. A tall, sturdily built, late middle-aged man emerged from the farmhouse behind the dog. Calham's grease-stained overalls, unkempt hair and ruddy complexion belied a sharp, steely glint in the man's eyes. The frowning farmer advanced on Matt, wiping his hands clean on a rag produced from his pocket.

"Help you?" said Calham.

"My car," said Matt. "My car broke down, back over there."

Calham looked him up and down with a severe stare.

"Lucky you found your way here then," he said. "There's not a lot of anything around this part of the country."

"You got that right," said Matt.

"Where were you heading?"

"Oh, nowhere in particular, I was just out for a Sunday drive, you know, see the countryside."

"Yeah?" said Calham. "Nice. Nice work if you can get it."

The collie continued a long, low, strained growl at Matt, before finally snapping at him. Matt flinched and took a step backwards.

"Do you mind?" said Matt.

"Don't mind him," said Calham. "Silly old thing. Duke! Inside!"

Duke crouched low under his master's harsh tone, before scampering back into the farmhouse. Calham looked sideways at Matt, continuing to eye his visitor suspiciously. He finished wiping his hands and pocketed the filthy rag.

"Have you got a phone I could borrow, please?" said Matt.

"No," said Calham. "No phone."

Matt looked around awkwardly, as the farmer's piercing eyes continued to bore through him.

"That's amazing corn you've got here," said Matt. "Late harvest?"

"This ground," said Calham. "Real fertile."

Matt's awkwardness was beginning to show. He looked back at the way he'd come into the farm, at the track through the woods, and then out over the surrounding landscape. He noticed heavy vehicle tracks behind the barns, heading out to the west.

"Does that lead out on to a road?" said Matt.

Calham stared at him.

"Eventually," he said.

Matt sighed quietly and began to back up towards the tracks and the exit.

"Well, thanks for the help," he said. "I'm sorry I disturbed you."

Matt quickly turned to follow the Land Rover's tracks, relieved to finally be on his way. Moments later the farmer called after him.

"Come on back," said Calham. "I'll run you to a garage in the Landy. Matt stopped and lingered at a distance, unsure how far he might dare to play out his cover story.

"I don't want to be any trouble," said Matt.

"No trouble," said Calham. "You'll just have to wait till I've eaten, that's all."

Matt looked longingly back down the tracks that bisected the cornfields and led out towards the road and eventual freedom.

"Not much traffic out here," said Calham. "You'll have a hell of walk to the next village."

Matt looked up at the farmhouse and then begrudgingly nodded to Calham with a forced smile. The farmer turned away and headed back inside without further word.

Matt reluctantly followed him in.

CHAPTER SEVEN

Matt stepped in through the back door and into a huge kitchen-cum-dining room. The low beams and antiquated furnishings made the room feel ancient, even for a farmer's kitchen. Calham gestured for Matt to take a seat at the huge, worn oak dining table that dominated the centre of the room. Matt sat and let his eyes roam around the glut of hoarded bric-a-brac cluttering the walls. Piles of faded magazines and old toys competed with rusted farm tools, dusty jars, bottles and mugs for scant shelf space. Calham filled a kettle from the sink and lit the gas on top of the stove with a match. He opened the oven to check on a roasting joint of beef, wafting warm air around the kitchen. Matt smelt the aroma of cooking meat mix with the old scent of musty papers, as his eyes fell on Duke, curled up in a basket in the corner. He began to lose himself again in his mind and the search for lost memories, trying to sift familiarity from fact.

"...and sugar?" said Calham.

"Sorry?" said Matt.

The burly farmer turned around from the kitchen work surface and fixed an impatient gaze on Matt.

"I said, milk and sugar?"

"Yes," said Matt. "Two please."

Calham brewed up two mugs of tea and put one down in front of Matt. He then returned to the sink and began washing plates and cutlery. Matt reached for the mug, but hesitated. He checked the farmer wasn't watching, then leaned forwards and inspected the tea, sniffing it. When he looked up again, he saw Calham silhouetted against the window, watching him closely. Matt's features began to redden, so he slowly took a sip of tea and winced.

"Hot," said Matt.

"Do you want some food to go with that?" said Calham.

"No," said Matt. "I'm fine, thanks."

Calham turned his attention back to the sink and resumed washing up plates, ignoring Matt's reply.

"I'll do you some," said Calham. "I've already cooked anyway."

The farmer emptied water from the washing up bowl and leaned back against the sink, drying more plates as he continued to watch Matt. Matt began to feel more and more uncomfortable under the weight of his host's silent stare.

"So," said Matt. "You always been a farmer?"

Calham nodded slowly.

"Is it just you?" said Matt.

Calham nodded again.

"It must be difficult. On your own. I mean, there's a lot of land."

"Oh, I don't work it like I used to," said Calham. He stacked the last dry plate with the others on the side and raised a long-bladed carving knife from the draining board. Matt watched nervously as the farmer began to carefully dry the blade with half a wry smile playing on his face.

"Let me ask you a question...err...?"

"Matt," said Matt. "Matt Sadler."

"...Mr. Sadler," continued Calham. "You ever been on a farm before?"

"No," said Matt. "Never."

"Then what the hell would you know about farming?"

Silence.

Matt looked anxiously from Calham's lazy smirk to the knife blade and back again. Calham began to quietly chuckle to himself. He put the dried knife on the side and coughed into his hand to halt his laughter.

Matt tensed up.

"Sorry, Mr. Sadler," said Calham. "I don't get many visitors. I know most you city fellas think farmers like me are gun-toting nut-jobs, that we shoot anyone stepping foot on our land."

"Well..."

"Like I said, I don't get many callers. Just having a little fun with you that's all."

Matt mustered a slight, nervous laugh, too late to sound convincing, and nodded in agreement. Calham picked up a far less threatening cluster of spoons and began drying them, suddenly looking relaxed, almost friendly.

"So where are you from, Matt?"

"Shrewsbury."

Calham nodded in reply and raised an eyebrow.

"Nice," he said. "Nice place."

Calham held Matt's gaze for slightly too long, before finally speaking again.

"So, what really brings you all the way out here?" he said. "You didn't break down, did you?"

Matt shifted uneasily in his chair.

"What makes you think that?"

"Well," said Calham. "I don't know any man that would be fool enough not to look under the bonnet of his car when he'd broken down, especially if it was out in the middle of nowhere without a phone. And your hands, Matt; your hands are as clean as a whistle."

Matt held his breath. He tried to think of something convincing to say, but couldn't.

"You said you didn't have a phone, right?"

Matt nodded a little too quickly.

"Well?" continued Calham.

"I was just out for a ride," said Matt. "Really."

Matt sighed and stared back at the farmer.

He didn't even sound convincing to himself.

What the hell. He had to tell someone; he was starting to go crazy.

"I've been having...episodes...blackouts." he began. "I'm not a heavy drinker, I don't use drugs..."

"So?" said Calham.

"Well, I had a feeling driving near here," said Matt. "Déjà vu or something. So I pulled over and started looking around. I thought maybe I'd been around here before. I followed a trail in the woods and popped out at your place."

Calham crossed his arms across his chest and leaned back against the sink thoughtfully.

"And have you?" said Calham. "Been round here before?"

"No," said Matt.

"Well, I'm no expert on these things," said Calham. "But it sounds like you should see a doctor."

"Now that phrase has got Déjà vu written all over it," said Matt.

Calham smiled and went back to drying the crockery matter of factly.

"Well," he said. "You might as well stay for something to eat anyway."

Matt wearily rose from his chair, feeling embarrassed. He made a show of stretching and affected a yawn. He glanced out through the kitchen window at the light failing outside.

"No thanks," said Matt. "I better be going. It's almost dark and I need to find my way back to the car."

"Fair enough," said Calham.

It was then that something caught Matt's eye in the far corner of the room. He immediately walked over to the tangle of wires and metal animal shapes dangling from the shelf, instantly transfixed by it. He lifted the child's mobile and let it hang straight out in front of him. Various outlines of ducks, cows, sheep, pigs and other farmyard animals, crudely rendered from sheet metal, began to twirl on their separate wires suspended from the mobile. Matt stared at the rotating shapes as they caught the dying light spilling in through the kitchen window.

"Cute," said Matt. "Did you make this?"

Calham appeared behind Matt, drying his hands on a tea towel. Matt was still completely focused on the cluster of twirling metal shapes, unsure of its significance, but certain that it meant something to him.

"Yeah," said Calham.

"Who's it for?" said Matt. "I thought you said you live alone?"

Matt's eye was then drawn to one of the metal silhouettes in particular; the figure of a farmer carrying a shotgun.

Then it hit him.

Matt suddenly knew he'd been here before.

No doubt about it.

Calham raised the carving knife from under the cover of the tea towel, as this thought fired in the younger man's brain. He stepped in behind Matt and quickly drew the blade across his throat.

A look of surprise hit Matt and his eyes grew wide as his throat opened up. Then his legs buckled beneath him, and he crumbled to the ground like a freshly slaughtered calf.

Matt lay there on his back, on the kitchen floor, with bright blood bubbling up from his sliced throat, hyperventilating, staring up at Calham in confusion. The farmer just stood over him, watching, shaking his head.

Finally, Calham knelt down over Matt's shivering body and raised the knife again.

"When will you learn to stay away?" he said, tutting.

Calham leaned forwards and abruptly drove the knife down hard into Matt's forehead, putting his whole weight on to it, until the blade was buried all the way up to the handle. Calham slowly stood up and returned to the sink, as Matt's dying body continued to tremble.

The farmer sipped his tea and stared out through the window across the fallow field. Behind him, Matt's body finally stopped twitching.

CHAPTER EIGHT

Calham trudged out over the sloping fallow field, as the sun began to sink into the horizon behind him, spilling red, dying light across Shadowbrook Farm. Matt's body hung over Calham's broad shoulder like a side of beef. In his free hand, the farmer carried a shovel. The slightest hum could be heard in the field, coming from beneath the soil, as if an electric current was coursing deep underground, competing with the steady, distant chug of the farm's generator, and the callous calls of the crows resting in the surrounding treetops. Calham stopped in the centre of the fallow field and let Matt's corpse slump to the ground. He dug the shovel into the strange earth there and began to carve out a shallow grave for his latest victim.

* * *

Blackness.

Somewhere in the distance a baby's screams gradually rose to fill Matt's ears, before slowly retreating and fading again. Even further beyond that, somewhere deeper in the infinite blackness, Matt was vaguely aware of the constant crackle of flames burning. The sound of the flames grew louder and louder, as if they were moving closer. Matt could not only hear the flames now, he could feel their heat searing him. Then the heat and the sound of the flames suddenly died away, and Matt felt himself rushing forwards through the cool, empty darkness. Rushing so fast that his consciousness failed him.

* * *

More blackness.

After several moments of quiet, there were more noises to be heard. Creaking hinges and the banging of a rickety wooden door. Heavy, clumping footsteps approached across a dirt floor and were followed by the sound of slack chains stirring and dragging. The blackness was suddenly ripped away, as a sackcloth hood was snatched up from Matt's face.

Matt's dazed eyes tried to focus on the tired, dirty wooden slats covering the inside of the barn. He looked down to see thick chains looped tightly around his wrists. His eyes followed the chain back up to see it pulled high and taught over a wooden beam above his head. Someone sighed directly behind Matt, and he felt the chain slacken off for a moment, as it quickly ran loose over the beam. Matt slumped and felt himself dropping, but large arms took his weight and prevented him from hitting the ground.

The figure behind Matt walked him over to a wooden chair in the centre of the barn that was positioned beneath a single light bulb hanging from a wire. The naked bulb illuminated only the immediate area around the chair, leaving the vague outlines of the surrounding crates and redundant farm machinery half realised in the shadows.

Calham dumped Matt into the chair and then circled around to look at him. The farmer's ruddy, red, inquisitive face hovered over him in the gloom. Matt's naked form doubled over in a coughing fit, as Calham knelt down next to him and secured his chains beneath the chair. Matt spat phlegm on to the straw-strewn floor and looked up blankly at his jailer.

Calham stood up and stepped back, surveying his handiwork.

"How do you feel?" said Calham.

"Terrible," said Matt. "Like I've been run over."

Calham smiled.

"Where am I?"

"You don't get to ask questions," said Calham.

Matt pulled against his chains, genuinely dumbfounded by the realization that he was bound. He looked up at Calham with a lost expression.

"Why am I...?" said Matt.

"Do you remember your name?" said Calham.

"Yes," said Matt. "It's..."

Calham began pacing backwards and forwards, watching Matt closely as he struggled to remember.

"...Matt," he said. "Matt Sadler."

"Good," said Calham. "What else do you remember, Matt Sadler?"

Matt stared into the ground and tried to concentrate.

"Driving," said Matt. "I was driving."

"And?" said Calham. "Do you remember the farm?"

Matt shook his head.

Calham moved closer and leaned down in front of him, staring into his eyes.

"Look at me," said Calham. "Do you remember me?"

Matt stared closely at the older man's dead eyes and pockmarked features. He slowly shook his head. Calham's own stare lingered longer on Matt, before he eventually rose and chuckled to himself.

"Oh," said Calham. "I'm sure you will though, eh? You remember everything eventually. Yeah. I'm going to have to keep a real close eye on you."

"You seem to know me pretty well," said Matt. "What's your name?"

"Calham," replied the farmer. "You must be hungry by now."

Matt's eyes lit up at the mention of food, as the farmer disappeared into the shadows at the rear of the barn. Calham reappeared moments later with a plastic bottle of water and a dog bowl. The latter was filled with what looked and smelt like dog food. Calham stood over Matt again and poured the water into his mouth, as Matt struggled to gulp down as much of it as he could. Calham then tossed aside the plastic bottle and held the bowl of dog food in front of Matt's face. Matt hesitated, looking down at the glutinous chunks of reformed meat, and then up at Calham. The hesitation didn't last though. Matt thrust his face into the dish and attacked it. Calham watched him eat hungrily, then pulled the dish away, making Matt instinctively crane his neck to follow it, still chewing. Calham put the bowl down on the ground and watched with amusement as Matt swallowed down the rest of the food.

"Get some rest," said Calham. "We've got a long day and an early start tomorrow."

Matt's eyes flared at this, and he tried to speak, but his mouth was still full, and Calham was already producing a hessian sack, fashioned into a hood. The farmer dropped the hood down over Matt's shaking head before he could swallow the food and speak up.

"No!" he said finally. "No, no!"

Calham ignored Matt's pleas and reached up over his head for the light cord dangling next to the bulb. He smiled to himself and pulled it, plunging the barn into darkness.

CHAPTER NINE

Somewhere in the distance, the baby began screaming its lungs out again. The blackness all around Matt gradually shifted and turned and faded, until it finally revealed mounds of tightly packed earth. The crumbling soil was suddenly visible all around him, moving closer and closer, packing in on him and squeezing against him, tumbling down over him, into his face and eyes. His hands flailed and dug, almost trying to swim out through the tons of falling earth without success. He could hear his own rasping, snatched breaths, each one becoming shorter than the last, as claustrophobia took hold. He could also hear the blood pounding inside his head, rising above the infant's screams. More and more earth slid towards him in an endless wave, as his hands tried desperately to push it all away. His last wheezing breath failed, and his tight lungs ached, as his air finally ran out. Matt's arms instinctively flailed against the crushing earth in panic, his hands attacking the approaching tide of soil.

Then a break.

Pure, blinding white light began to spill through a breach in the dirt. His hands quickly clawed at the earth around the gap, feeling it give, crumble and break apart. More bright light poured in through the cracks, blinding Matt, as he gasped and managed to fill his lungs with air again.

* * *

The sun rose over Shadowbrook Farm and began burning through a thick blanket of early morning mist. Shadows slowly retreated across the farmyard, chased away by the advancing morning. Shafts of sunlight spilled through the plethora of cracks in the barn's creaking woodwork. Matt, naked and still hooded and chained, began to stir. He sensed a presence and jerked his head about trying to find its source.

Calham quietly opened the barn door and crept up on his blind prisoner.

"Hello?" said Matt. "Hello?"

Calham silently watched him for a moment, before unlocking the chains at the back of his chair.

"Stand," said Calham.

Matt stood, still hooded and confused. Calham then led him away by the chain, walking him out of the barn like livestock. He led Matt outside and over to the Land Rover. He secured Matt's chain to the vehicle's grill, then pulled the hood from his head. Matt flinched, squinting at the bright sunlight. Duke the dog warily approached Matt and began sniffing around the earth next to his feet. Matt instinctively backed away from the dog. A moment later it recognised his scent, looked up at Matt and began to growl. Calham watched the two of them with idle interest.

"Going to be a hot one today," he said.

Calham threw a set of dirty overalls at Matt. Matt automatically picked them up and stepped into them, pulling them up awkwardly with his chained hands, his blank mind following some unconscious thread of buried, learned behaviour . He watched Calham plod back into the barn. The farmer reappeared moments later with a large roll of plastic sheeting balanced on his shoulder and a child's dirt-stained backpack. Matt watched Calham dump both in the back of the Land Rover, before returning to the barn. When he reappeared for the second time, Calham was wearing protective gloves and carrying a large roll of barbed wire. Tucked under his other arm were a cluster of fence posts and a lump hammer. Matt continued to watch, as all of this gear was slung into the back of the Land Rover too. Matt's right hand flinched and cramped up, distracting him. He tried to straighten and hold the shaking hand steady, as it tried to spasm and knot up again. Calham slammed the back of the Land Rover shut and approached Matt brandishing a double barrel shotgun.

"You look a little shaky," said Calham.

"Where are you taking me?" said Matt.

"You're on a farm now. So you've got a full day's work ahead of you."

Calham took off his work gloves and tossed them into the Land Rover through the window. He reached for the chain that tied Matt to the grill and then thought better of it. Instead, he leaned in close to Matt and raised the shotgun, pushing the muzzle up under his chin.

"You ever see what one of these can do?"

"No," said Matt.

"They don't call them scatter guns for nothing," said Calham. "You better not mess me about."

Matt nodded slowly.

Calham then carefully reached behind him, his eyes never leaving Matt's, and unlocked the chain.

"Get in," said Calham.

Matt slowly climbed into the passenger side and patiently waited while Calham tethered his hands with the chain again. Calham climbed in behind the wheel, stowed the shotgun between his seat and the door, and started her up.

Calham fiddled with the radio as they pulled away, but all he could find out here in the wilderness was the rise and fall of empty static, and a ghostly whining bleeding through the airwaves. The farmer left it on anyway. The Land Rover headed out across the farm and cut along the track between the cornfields to leave.

The Land Rover wound its way along a succession of twisting country lanes, through forests and fields, as the spectral static on the radio continued to rise and fall. Eventually the Land Rover rounded a tight bend following the edge of a forest and pulled off the country lane to roll to a stop under the cover of trees. Calham got out and climbed up a steep, grass-covered slope to a small hill overlooking the road. Watching from the Land Rover, Matt could just make out Calham, as he took a pair of binoculars out of his backpack and began surveying the surrounding landscape. He used them to track the curve of the empty road and followed its route in both directions as it followed the treeline. Calham then slung the binoculars around his neck again and looked over the rest of the hill, and at the cover afforded by the surrounding trees. He stared up at the blazing sun and wiped sweat away from his leaking brow with his sleeve. He sighed and made his way back down the slope to the Land Rover. He opened Matt's door and unlocked his prisoner's chains, before motioning with the shotgun for Matt to climb out too.

Calham marched Matt up the slope and through the trees, prodding him with the shotgun as they climbed. He steered Matt towards a last lone tree before a clearing, a gnarly oak situated about halfway up, and made him stand with his back against its trunk. Calham then looped Matt's chain around one of the thicker low branches and secured it tightly.

Calham left Matt tethered to the oak, undercover, but with a clear vantage point of the bend in the road below. Matt pulled down on the chain, testing the branch's resistance, but it was solid, and he realised any escape attempt would be futile. Feeling helpless, he turned his attention back to Calham, who was now down at the foot of the slope again, reversing the Land Rover out of its cover and back out on to the road. Calham then stopped it again and got out. He began unloading the fence posts and barbed wire at the side of the road. Once he was finished, he climbed back into the Land Rover and returned it to its former position under the cover of the tree canopy.

Matt watched Calham with curiosity, as the farmer emerged from the trees moments later, carrying just the child's backpack. Calham sauntered along the side of the road in the sunshine and picked up one of the fence posts. He drove it into the ground and then lifted the lump hammer. He heaved the hammer against the stake, driving it deep into the ground with a heavy pounding. Matt watched the farmer slog away, striking the stake three more times, before setting to work on the roll of wire fencing. Calham produced a small Stanley knife from his pocket and cut away the binding from the barbed wire. He positioned the wire ready to roll out by the side of the road. The farmer then turned and stared directly up at Matt, catching him watching. The older man held Matt's gaze, as he slipped the backpack over his shoulder and began to climb back up the slope again. Calham ascended and stopped in open ground, a few metres away from Matt, where he sat down. He delved into the backpack and pulled out a pair of thick-framed sunglasses and a sports cap. He put them on, looking anything but cool. Calham then rose again and strode over to where Matt was shackled. Matt braced himself and tried to back away as Calham advanced on him. The farmer reached into his overall pockets and pulled out a dirty rag. He playfully twirled it around with his finger at Matt, then leaned in closer and gagged the younger man with it.

Satisfied that everything was as it should be, Calham strolled back to his spot further down the slope and sat down. Matt watched him pick up the binoculars and begin casually scanning the road again, searching for his next victim.

CHAPTER TEN

Matt watched the midday sun beat down on Calham as he swigged water from a large plastic bottle. The big man then lit a cigarette and stretched out on the grass as if this were an idle lunchtime in the park. Matt eyed him jealously from the shade of the tree, where he was anything but comfortable. He looked like a marionette suspended from the branches with all but one string cut. His chained arms hung from the thickest branch directly above his head, while the full weight of his aching body slumped awkwardly against the trunk, his feet just touching the ground. The enforced stretch through his shoulders and chest was the worst, he felt as if he was slowly being wrenched apart by his own body weight. He noticed Calham sit up for a moment and casually check both ways along the road below them with the binoculars, before looking up at the sun. He pushed his cap up and dabbed away the sweat beneath with a rag. Sighing, the farmer stood up and moved closer to Matt, planting himself down beneath the shade of the tree too. He lay back down on the grass, interlocking his fingers behind his head for support as he appeared to nap.

* * *

Calham propped himself up on one elbow and lazily scanned the road below with his binoculars again. Matt continued to watch him, but his eyes were no longer focusing properly. His weary head rolled about on his taut shoulders, as pain, fatigue and dehydration took their toll.

Calham suddenly sat bolt upright. He raised the binoculars and his head slowly turned to track the movement of a distant vehicle. He followed a dirty white van with two workmen in the front speeding towards the bend in the road. Calham then visibly relaxed and lowered the binoculars, having no intention of tackling the two men. He reached over and delved into his backpack instead, pulling out a plastic tub of food. He opened it and unwrapped a stack of homemade cheese sandwiches. He munched on them, unconcerned, as the white van passed by on the road below.

Matt caught sight of the sandwiches and straightened up. He watched Calham closely, his own hunger growing with each bite taken. Calham finished the sandwiches and then bit into a ripe, red apple. He could hear the chain rubbing against bark behind him, as Matt shuffled about, now desperate with hunger. Calham took another bite and then casually tossed the apple over his shoulder. It landed at Matt's feet, where he could only stare at it longingly. Calham casually wiped his mouth with his sleeve and stood. He sauntered over to Matt and looked him up and down, smiling at his predicament. The farmer then slackened off the chain and removed Matt's gag, making him groan in both pain and relief, as he fell to the ground. He watched in faint amusement as the younger man scrabbled on his knees for the half-eaten apple and began scoffing it. Calham lit up a cigarette and watched Matt snort and attack the apple like a ravenous hog.

"Water," said Matt. "Have you got any water?"

Calham reached into his backpack and tossed him the plastic bottle. Matt immediately upended it, greedily glugging down the warm water inside. Calham stepped forwards and took the bottle from him before he finished it. He casually belted Matt across the face with the back of his large hand and the younger man crumpled to the ground. Calham screwed the cap back on the bottle and took another drag of his cigarette.

"I've kept pigs with more grace than you," he said.

The farmer suddenly frowned, and his whole face appeared to crease in concentration. He turned back towards the road and grabbed his binoculars again.

Sure enough, there, in the distance, was a car heading towards them.

Calham licked his lips as he stared through the lenses. Then he was off and moving surprisingly quickly for a man his size, running behind the tree and hauling on the chain, forcing Matt to howl in pain as he was jerked back upwards, strung up tight against the branch overhead again. Calham quickly stuffed the gag back into Matt's mouth and then hurried away down the slope, snatching up his backpack on the way. As he jogged down the hill, he took his work gloves from the backpack and pulled them over his hands. At the foot of the hill, he headed straight for the loose coils of barbed wire and grabbed the roll, steering it and rolling out the wire, so that it lay across the narrow road.

Matt looked on anxiously, as Calham then ran back over to the side of the road and quickly planted another fence post in the ground. As the car approached the blind bend from the other side of the hill, Calham slipped a small, dark bottle into his overall pocket from the backpack. He then began to busy himself with the lump hammer and the fence stake.

A new 4x4 took the bend at speed and abruptly skidded to a halt, as the driver saw the barbed wire stretched across the road and jammed on the brakes. Its locked wheels stopped just short of the spiky coils covering the asphalt.

Calham didn't even bother to look around.

The vehicle's horn blared impatiently.

Calham paid it no attention.

The driver's side window slid down and a young woman's face peered out. She glared at the barbed wire lying across the road and then at Calham, who still had his back to her.

"What the hell are you doing?" she shouted.

Calham ignored her, striking the top of the fence post with the hammer again. The woman seethed at his ignorance and narrowed her eyes.

"Hey, you," she said. "You're blocking the road with this stuff."

Calham slowly turned to meet her gaze. He was wearing the sunglasses now and his cap was pulled down tightly over his head. He dropped the hammer and walked towards the side of her vehicle.

Matt tried to shout, to warn the woman, but his desperate cries were no more than muted mumbles and moans absorbed by the gag in his mouth. He shook his head in despair, waiting for the scene to unfold, powerless to influence it in any way.

"You could have killed me leaving that stuff all over the road," said the woman. "It's bloody idiotic."

Calham reached the side of the vehicle and just stared solemnly at the woman. He watched her face tighten, as she suddenly digested the reality of the situation she was in, noting Calham's brutish appearance and proximity. She swallowed her next words and quickly shrank back into her seat, now trembling. Her eyes dropped to the inside of her door, searching for the locking button and the window's controls.

But it was already too late.

Calham quickly stepped in close to the door and his arm shot through the open window. His large handheld a dirty rag which he pushed against her mouth, smothering her with it, as she kicked and thrashed and flailed, all to no avail. Her eyes bulged with panic, as she felt the chloroform drowning her senses. Then she seized and stiffened, and then finally slumped back down into her seat. Calham opened up the door and released the woman's dead weight from her safety belt. He then slid her over to the passenger seat and climbed in behind the wheel.

Matt watched Calham put the 4x4 in reverse and drive it back up off the lane and under the cover of trees next to his own Land Rover. Matt struggled to maintain his view of the vehicle, snatching only intermittent glimpses of Calham hauling the woman out of it and moving her. The farmer threw the woman in the back of the Land Rover, quickly rolling her in the heavy sheets of black plastic there. He then took the wheel again and pulled the Land Rover back out on to the road, stopping it next to the sprawling coils of barbed wire. Matt looked on, as Calham carefully rolled the wire back up, then collected up the fence posts, and threw it all in the back of the Land Rover, on top of the rolled plastic and the unfortunate woman wrapped inside. Calham then climbed back into the Land Rover and reversed it under the tree line again, disappearing completely from Matt's line of sight this time.

Matt looked down the slope and over the ambush site there. It now seemed normal again, like any other stretch of country road, devoid of any evidence of the abduction that had just taken place. He blinked and looked up at the sky, wondering if any of this was in fact real, or if it was just another fantastic nightmare conjured by his broken mind. The jet trail of a passenger plane streaking high overhead caught his eye. He craned to watch it, struck by the normality it represented in this strange new universe he'd found himself trapped in. He felt jealous of the occupants inside the plane, making their escape to places unknown. Making their escape to anywhere.

Calham appeared beside Matt, holding the shotgun braced against his hip.

"I bet you thought I'd forgotten about you," he said.

Calham unhooked the chain from the branch above Matt and pulled it taught like a leash. Leaving the gag stuffed in Matt's mouth, he walked his captive down through the sloping woodland to the waiting Land Rover below.

CHAPTER ELEVEN

As they drove back to Shadowbrook Farm, Matt sat passively in the passenger seat, staring straight ahead. He continued to stare at the country lanes that rolled by, reflected in the Land Rover's windows. Calham bit into another apple, as he handled the wheel and looked across at his unwilling accomplice. The farmer's eyes darted back and forth between Matt and the rear-view mirror. Calham then smiled to himself as he realised Matt was not staring out through the windshield, but deep into the rear-view mirror; staring at the reflection of an inert shape wrapped in black plastic and covered in loops of barbed wire.

    The bouncing Land Rover cut back along the dirt track between the cornfields surrounding Shadowbrook Farm, as a swollen sun began to set against the nearby hills. They pulled up between the two barns near the farmhouse and Calham climbed out. Without looking at Matt, he began to unload the back of the Land Rover. Matt solemnly watched the farmer carry the fence posts and then the wire back into the barn where he had spent the previous night. Calham then returned and heaved the heavy roll of plastic containing the woman on to his shoulders. He marched this over to the second barn instead and unlocked the door there, before disappearing inside. Matt looked out over the woodland on the horizon and watched the sun slowly sink and melt into the trees. Moments later he flinched, as a hand yanked the gag out of his mouth. He turned to see Calham's grinning face at the open window next to him.

Calham peered back over his shoulder at the second barn, light now spilling out through its open doorway.

"You ready?" he said.

* * *

Calham led a reluctant Matt into the second barn by his chain. Matt's blood froze when he entered this building for the first time and saw a long grid of blood-stained chicken wire nailed across the back wall. They shuffled through a layer of sawdust on the floor, past a large tool rack laden with an erratic mixture of gleaming farm, factory and surgical appliances. Drill bits sat next to pitchforks, G-clamps, hacksaws, axes and scalpel blades. All were in superb condition, sharp and shining, a sharp contrast to the dingy surroundings of the barn's interior.

"This is the workshop," said Calham. "This is where we get down to the nitty-gritty."

He led Matt through a makeshift partition, assembled from bales of stacked hay, to where most of the light was concentrated. Here, beneath a cluster of florescent strips, lay a huge, old wooden workbench. Restrained on top of its scarred surface was the woman from the 4x4, still unconscious.

Matt stared at her in horror, as Calham chained his hands through a metal ring, bolted to the barn floor. Calham then slipped his jacket off and began to roll his sleeves up ready for work. His face was now red and alive with sweat and anticipation. Matt watched him prepare excitedly, before looking down at the work bench again. He reached out and ran his fingers over its gnarled and chipped surface, wondering how many other victims had lay here before. Something stirred deep inside Matt and he instinctively looked up at the strip lighting overhead. This was the same view someone strapped to the workbench would have seen. The lights began to slide out of focus and Matt suddenly felt woozy, crumpling down against the ground. He sat there on the ground in a daze. Calham stared down at him and chuckled, shaking his head in disappointment.

"Please," said Matt. "Whatever it is you're going to do, don't."

Calham just grinned at him and produced a large Stanley knife. He extended the blade, then advanced on the sleeping woman.

"Please," said Matt. "Don't."

Calham cut into the bottom of the smartly dressed woman's trouser leg and gradually drew the blade up, slashing the material open. The farmer turned and looked at Matt with mischievous raised eyebrows, before going to work on the top section of her clothing. Matt swallowed hard, as the farmer cut through the woman's underwear and slid it away too. Calham stared at Matt and made a pantomime of using her severed bra and pants to mop away a feverish sweat from his brow. He then reached into his pocket and retrieved a small capsule. He leaned in close over the naked woman, savouring her smell and appearance. He then winked at Matt.

"Time to go to work," he said.

Calham broke the capsule under the woman's nose, making her instantly flinch and pull away. Her eyes fluttered open and fixed on Calham. She remained silent, and for a moment there was no sound save the slow chug of the farm's generator and the hum of the fluorescent tubes overhead. The woman's wide, confused eyes then swivelled around, drinking in as much of the surrounding scene as her restricted point of view allowed.

Then the screaming started.

High and hysterical, the woman screamed as loudly as she could. She wavered only to snatch more air with which to further fuel her desperate lungs. Calham circled the work bench, unconcerned, then headed back through the partition in the direction of the tool rack. The screaming brought Matt's senses back into the here and now. He rose and tried to lean forwards and see what Calham was up to in the back, but he couldn't reach far enough to see. His movement made the woman stop screaming. She fixed her gaze on him for a moment and sat up as far as her tie-wrapped arms would allow.

"Please," she said. "Please, you've got to help me."

Matt shook his head.

"Please help me," said the woman. "I don't want to die. Please don't let him hurt me, please..."

Matt tried to raise his hands, showing her the chains that tethered him to the ring in the floor at the foot of the workbench.

"I'm sorry," he said. "I'm so sorry..."

Tears welled up in both captives' eyes. The woman then screwed hers shut and lay back down. She began to bang the back of her head against the bench's surface and let out a long, mournful wail. Calham strolled back into the workshop with a handful of scalpels of different sizes and a hacksaw.

His casual manner couldn't hide the greedy malice shining in his eyes as he approached the workbench.

"Don't do this..." said Matt.

Calham no longer noticed Matt. He scattered the surgical instruments out on a black cloth laid over one of the hay bales and selected a large scalpel.

He then slowly moved in towards the workbench. The sobbing woman, her eyes still closed, instinctively turned away as she felt his hot breath on her body. Matt watched Calham raise the scalpel and then he turned away too.

CHAPTER TWELVE

Somewhere in the blackness, Matt heard the sound of a sharp slap landing on a face. It took him a moment or two to realise it was in fact his face. Another slap followed, stinging his groggy features, forcing his eyes open. This blow left blood smeared across his cheek. He groaned and stared up at Calham. The wild-eyed farmer was panting like a dog without water, and looked like he'd been painted red from head to toe. Matt could just about see the woman behind him, still lying on the workbench. She was still partially obscured by the burly farmer, but Matt could hear her delirious moans, and see that the workbench was awash with blood too. Calham took deep breaths to calm himself in the aftermath of his apparent frenzy. He appeared to slowly return his focus to the here and now, his face gradually relaxing, as he came down from his former state of ecstasy. He looked at his watch and his expression tightened again. He grabbed a butcher's knife and headed back towards the workbench, suddenly infused with a sense of urgency.

"Get up," he snapped at Matt. "We don't have long."

Matt rose on wobbly legs, his head rushing, and looked up just in time to see Calham raise the injured woman's head from the workbench and casually slit her throat. Matt instantly whirled away from the scene and vomited across the floor. Calham tutted to himself and shook his head. He used the knife to cut away the remaining tie wraps from the dead woman's hands and feet, and then approached Matt. The farmer stood over him, watching him dry heave, a smug sense of superiority on his bloody face. After a moment he reached down and slapped the younger man's back.

"Come on now," he said. "That's enough."

Matt stood up and coughed, spitting bile. He heard the sound of chain links dragging and looked down to see that his hands were now free. His eyes then returned to Calham, only to find the farmer's shotgun already pointing at him. Calham slowly panned it towards the woman's body.

"Get that," he said.

Matt looked at the woman's red, abused body and instantly backed away, shaking his head. He didn't want to touch it. Calham pushed the shotgun closer, thumbing back the hammers. Matt took a deep breath and reluctantly approached the workbench. He hesitated, then, with some awkwardness and effort, picked up the slippery corpse in his arms and turned to face Calham. The farmer smiled back at him and pointed the shotgun towards the door to show him the way. A dark red stain began to spread across Matt's chest as he carried the woman's body towards the barn's exit.

"Good boy," said Calham.

Matt stared through the darkness, as he was forced to carry the dead woman ahead of Calham. It all felt unreal to him, as if he were somehow both awake and asleep at the same time, treading some preordained path, an actor forced to play his role without deviation, following his instructions to the letter. The farmer followed at his rear, pausing just once, to pocket a Maglite and grab a shovel, and then they both marched out of the building and into the night, making their way towards the fallow field.

* * *

Calham and Matt trudged through the fallow field in the darkness, following Calham's torch beam as it glided back and forth, guiding their route forwards over the resting earth. Matt wavered in the moonlight under the weight of the woman and the rising nausea in his gut. The torch beam ahead of them finally came to rest, hovering over an indistinct patch of grass.

"This'll do," said Calham.

Matt gently lay the woman's torn body on the ground, as if it were still vulnerable to further harm in some way. He then looked at Calham, waiting for some order or signal as to his next move. The farmer obliged, throwing the shovel down at his feet without a word. Matt wearily picked it up and began to dig, with the glare of the torch beam aimed squarely in his eyes.

* * *

Matt had dug nearly two feet down into the fresh grave and was beyond exhausted. Calham stayed back in the darkness watching him work, nothing more than an indistinct presence in the blackness behind the torch's glare.

"That's deep enough," he said. "Just a little broader at the sides."

As Matt laboured, Calham rested his torch on the mound of freshly turned earth at the side of the grave and struck a match. He lit a cigarette and sighed to himself.

"We never could get anything to grow in this field," he said. "Deadest soil I've ever seen."

For a moment, the farmer seemed lost to nostalgia, but then he quickly snapped back to the present.

"That's enough," he said.

Matt climbed out of the shallow grave, stood at the side and waited. The tip of Calham's cigarette flared against the darkness as he pulled on it again. Then the orange glow flitted out to the side, as Calham motioned with his hand towards the body. Matt hesitated, then took hold of the woman and gently rolled her down into the waiting hole. He looked over at Calham again, before starting to shovel soil over the dead woman's features.

"Yep," said Calham. "That's all we thought it was fit for. Cemetery soil."

Calham pulled on his cigarette one last time and flicked it into the open grave with the woman's corpse. Matt glared at him with naked contempt. He held the stare for as long as he dared, then returned to his labour, covering the glowing butt with earth. Calham raised his torch and angled the beam directly into Matt's eyes as he finished toiling, reminding him who was in charge.

CHAPTER THIRTEEN

A haggard-looking Matt trudged back towards the lights of the farmhouse, followed at a distance by Calham, who kept both shotgun barrels levelled squarely at his back. The farmer steered Matt into the barn where he'd been incarcerated and pointed with the shotgun to a straw-littered bedding area set against the wall. Matt complied blankly and stood on the straw and waited. Calham took a length of chain and a padlock from the empty chair in the centre of the barn and tossed them to Matt. Matt took the hint and began to run the chain through the spread of chicken wire behind him.

"Ah ah ah," said Calham.

He shook his head and pointed to a thick wooden support beam standing next to Matt. Matt reluctantly unlaced the chain and fed it around the much sturdier beam instead.

"The feet this time," said Calham. "Tight."

Matt sat and looped the chain tightly around both of his ankles and secured it with the padlock. Calham nodded, satisfied with the job, and then headed out of the barn. As soon as he was out of sight, Matt went to work on his foot, trying desperately to squeeze the chain over his ankle.

But there was no way.

He cursed under his breath and repeatedly hammered on the support beam with a clenched fist. Tears of frustration began to well in his eyes, and he snivelled and wiped them on his sleeve. When he looked up again through watery eyes, he saw that

Calham had quietly returned and was now standing over him, watching.

"I've seen it," said Matt. "I've seen what you do now. So why don't you just get it over with?"

Calham squatted down next to Matt, the way he might do to reassure a sick animal. In his hands he held the dead woman's bundled clothes.

"You're not going to let me go," said Matt. "Are you?"

Calham dropped the clothes into Matt's lap. He then leaned forward and stuck a small sowing needle, attached to a reel of black cotton, into Matt's thigh. Matt yelped and quickly pulled the needle out.

"Really small, careful stitches," said Calham. "On the inside, so it's not obvious."

Calham dropped a reel of white cotton into Matt's lap.

"You'll need this too," he said.

Matt forlornly watched Calham swagger back across the barn and leave for real this time.

* * *

Somewhere in that vast blackness, Matt could hear the baby screaming again.

* * *

Matt jerked awake. He was slumped against the barn wall with the woman's clothes and sowing kit still in his lap. The sun's rays pierced the gaps in the side of the barn and streamed in to create a dust-flecked latticework of light crisscrossing its interior. The barn door creaked open and Calham entered. He walked over to a dark corner nearby and opened a rusted old metal cabinet, then began to tinker there in the shadows with his back to Matt. He finally slammed the cabinet shut and approached Matt with two bowls of dog food. The farmer had a casual expression on his face that almost implied the events of the night before never took place.

"Morning," said Calham.

He placed one of the bowls down next to Matt and picked up the woman's clothes with his free hand. He glanced over the needlework and gave a noncommittal grunt, before heading back out with the other bowl of food. Matt watched him leave, his eyes following the other bowl in the farmer's hand.

* * *

Outside, Matt relieved himself against the side of the barn, as Calham lazily watched over him with the shotgun. Calham then marched him out over the fallow field at gunpoint. The familiar hum of latent, buried energy rose up to greet them as they climbed the gentle slope. Matt noticed a hessian sack hanging from the back of Calham's belt.

"You sickos like your early starts, don't you," said Matt.

"It's a farm," said Calham.

Matt grinned to himself, then his expression hardened.

"Can you hear that?" he said.

Calham remained silent.

"Nothing," he said. "No birds. Not even this early. You must have one hell of a scarecrow."

"Don't need one," said Calham. "Here."

Matt looked up and saw they were approaching the shovel that had been left sticking out of ground following the woman's hurried burial the night before. It leaned out of the plot at an angle like a crude, fallen cross. The two men stopped and Calham carefully circled the grave, examining the soil there. Matt looked down at the ground too, where the earth had been freshly turned the night before.

Where they buried the woman.

Matt stared at Calham with dark eyes.

The farmer, in turn, seemed to be scanning Matt's features, trying to read them.

"What the fuck is this?" said Matt.

"I thought that would take the wind out of your sails," said Calham.

Calham moved closer, his piercing eyes now smiling at Matt.

"Dig," he whispered.

Matt looked down at the exposed earth and then back at Calham. He slowly shook his head.

"Carefully," said Calham. "With your hands."

"No," said Matt.

Calham raised the shotgun and aimed it at Matt, but the younger man just stared back defiantly.

Calham slowly advanced, pushing the muzzle under Matt's jaw, then forcing it up. Matt didn't relent and didn't take his eyes off him. Calham thumbed back the hammer, raising the stakes.

Fuck it, thought Matt.

He grimaced and closed his eyes, bracing himself for the end.

For a moment, nothing.

Then Matt opened his eyes again, in time to see Calham taking a step back.

"So, the man's finally had enough and is ready to die..." said Calham. "...but what if I were to tell you there's hope? Would you be scared then?"

Confusion then curiosity lit up in Matt's eyes, followed quickly by fear. Calham gestured again with the shotgun for him to dig. Slowly, reluctantly, Matt advanced towards the grave and dropped to his knees. He carefully began to push aside the earth with his hands. He smelt a rank odour escaping into the air as he clawed more and more soil away. He had to fight the urge to heave.

Calham took a cigar from his pocket and bit off the tip, spitting it to the ground. He struck a match and evenly lit the cigar, as he watched Matt work the soil. The pungent smell released into the air was so bad now that Matt had to turn his head away as his fingers explored the earth.

"Yep," said Calham. "Didn't have much of a use for this field. Not until old Duke died..."

Matt flinched as his fingers touched something wet and slippery beneath the ground. Calham exhaled a plume of smoke and sighed with knowing satisfaction. Matt forced himself to look closely at the earth in front of him. He saw something viscous there, something slick and moist glistening beneath the top layer of dirt. He hesitated and then delved his hands into the sticky soil again.

"...and we decided to bury him out here." said Calham.

Matt's eyes opened wide as he gripped the unseen thing before him and slowly pulled it from the earth like some strange, unholy crop.

"Yep," said Calham. "That's the look I had on my face the first time I saw it."

Matt lifted it free of the soil, staring at it in disbelief. He wiped away the earth and blood and mucus from its face. The woman's features were groggy, confused, slick with a thick coating of embryonic mucus, but she was very much alive.

Calham took the hessian sack from his belt and slipped it over the woman's blank features. He then pulled her all the way out of her shallow grave and up to her feet. She rose automatically, complying like a tired child with its parent; though she apparently found it difficult to stand on her trembling, weakened legs. Calham held her steady and watched Matt, waiting for him to react to his homegrown miracle.

But Matt was barely aware of the farmer's mind games. He was quickly slipping into a dazed stupor, retreating to somewhere deep and dark and safe within himself. Calham frowned, unhappy at being denied the pleasure of seeing Matt confused and astounded and struggling to understand. He gruffly hauled Matt to his feet. Matt's head swam again with intense nausea and disbelief, until he finally doubled up and puked. Calham slapped his back to fetch it all up as he clawed at the ground. When Matt was done, Calham gently pushed him and the hooded woman back down the slope in the direction of the farmhouse.

CHAPTER FOURTEEN

Calham steered Matt and the hooded woman through their shared daze towards the second of the two dilapidated barns that stood near the farmhouse; the one that Matt had not yet been into. The interior was almost pitch black to Matt as they entered. Calham and the woman were rendered just vague, shuffling outlines moving against the dark. A single fluorescent strip light flickered into life and revealed Calham holding its dangling cord. Matt could now see that they were both standing on a bed of straw, cocooned in the fluorescent strip's small sphere of light against the surrounding darkness. Matt looked on numbly, as Calham lowered the hooded woman on to a makeshift bed of bundled blankets. She automatically sat down in a trance-like state among a collection of raggedy old stuffed toys arranged on there. One-eyed teddy bears and rat-nibbled fluffy animals stared back at Matt from the bedding like carefully arranged toy corpses. Calham plumped up the blankets for the woman as she sat, showing a strange restraint completely at odds with his previous behaviour. He then reached into the surrounding straw and pulled out leather straps that seemed to be attached to the floorboards beneath. He secured the straps around the woman's ankles and wrists, taking care not to fasten them too tightly.

"Wouldn't want to leave any marks now, would we?" he said.

Matt slowly began to back away, shaking his head, denying the scene, refusing this inversion of the laws of nature.

Calham turned and watched him retreat into the shadows.

"Where are you going?" said Calham.

Matt's face was as blank as his mind; it was all too much for him. His empty features disappeared, as he slid into the shadows at the far side of the barn.

"Hey," said Calham. "Don't go back there, I'm warning you."

Matt felt his way through the cloying darkness surrounding him, no longer caring about anything other than being as far away from this place as possible. He stumbled on something, but quickly regained his footing and carried on. It was then that he heard the sounds of chains dragging against wood up ahead.

Chains much heavier than the ones he was shackled with.

Somewhere in the distant recesses of his mind he heard Calham's voice call to him again. This time there was a genuine sense of urgency in the other man's voice.

"Stay where you are, Matt." yelled Calham. "Don't take another step."

Calham's tone made Matt falter and hesitate, even in his shell-shocked state. Then he heard the shuffling of something large nearby, as heavy chains scraped across floorboards towards him. Matt began to tremble, as thick, laboured breaths wheezed their way out of something waiting in the blackness up ahead. The whole barn suddenly flickered, as the remaining overhead fluorescent strips tried to flutter into life. Matt caught fleeting glimpses of the horror standing directly in front of him. The misshapen beast phased in and out of existence in the strobing light. Then it launched itself forwards. Matt scrabbled backwards, as the snarling, bulbous-headed creature lunged for him, swiping with gnarly, outstretched hands; but it was held at bay by a taught chain stretched between the collar around its neck and the wall behind it.

"Henry!" said Calham. "No!"

Matt quickly pushed himself further backwards across the floor and away from Henry, as Calham rushed towards him. The farmer grabbed Matt under his arms and dragged him away to safety.

"Get back in there, Henry," said Calham. "Settle down."

The growling thing called Henry relented. The silhouette of its huge foetus-like head on a gangling, twisted body of knotted muscle reluctantly slipped back into the shadows, as the overhead lights continued to flicker and fail. Matt caught snatches of Henry's wild, protruding eyes fixed on him, before they too were absorbed by the darkness in the far corner of the barn. Matt watched the last slack coil of thick chain slide away and disappear into the shadows too. Matt continued to stare, expecting the thing to re-emerge; but it didn't. He could now see more dirty soft toys scattered across the floor in the flickering light, or what was left of them; decapitated teddy bears and torn bunnies lying around the mouth of Henry's dark lair. A water bowl sat there too, along with the corner of a thick, pink, muddied blanket.

Calham leaned in over Matt and shook his head in mock despair.

"Another step," he said. "And I'd have been scrubbing this barn for a week."

Calham helped Matt up and walked him back towards the door.

"Henry's a messy eater," he said.

CHAPTER FIFTEEN

The fallow field continued to emit a low hum at ground level in the fading light of the late afternoon. The vibrations were strongest around the freshly dug mound of earth the woman had been pulled from, the breach still ebbing its strange energy. The wind picked up around the farm, stirring the high corn in the adjacent fields, folding it and forcing it back and forth in a hypnotic swaying motion. Calham and Matt emerged from the furthest barn and made their way over to the farmhouse, Matt walking in a daze as the farmer held his chain.

Once inside the kitchen, Matt sat down at the table without waiting for invitation or instruction, unaware of what happened to him the last time he was there. Calham tethered the chain around his waist to one of the heavy table's struts and padlocked it. Duke the dog eyed Matt suspiciously from his basket, his head low, his expression surly.

Matt looked around the cluttered walls and shelves of the kitchen, but only the vaguest feelings of familiarity washed over him. He watched Calham fill the kettle and boil it on the stove, preparing two mugs of tea. Matt rubbed his forehead and pinched the corners of his eyes against the bridge of his nose, trying to disperse a dull ache swelling where dozens of questions were trapped behind the nullifying sensation of shock. He slumped back in his chair and watched Calham put one of the mugs down in front of him. The farmer took the seat opposite him.

"Get that down you," said Calham. "You'll feel better."

"What was that thing?" said Matt.

Calham hesitated.

"Henry," he said.

"But what was it?" said Matt. "And the woman?"

"Calham sipped at his tea and pondered the question, before sighing an answer.

"The field always brings them back," he said. "But sometimes...sometimes they turn. Spoil. I don't know why exactly. The length of time you leave them in the ground has something to do with it. Leave them in too long and it's bad. And where you plant them matters too. Some parts of the field work better than others. Some parts don't do nothing at all. Anyway, if it goes wrong...then...then they come out like poor Henry. All twisted."

"It's a monster," said Matt. "Why don't you get rid of it?"

Calham shrugged his shoulders and looked down at the dog curled up in the corner.

"Same reason I keep old Duke," he said.

Matt took a deep breath and closed his eyes. Everything was muddled, confused. He didn't know what was real anymore. There were gaping holes in his mind and the farmer's tall tales weren't helping him fill them. There had been a murder, the woman had died, but now she was back. The farmer said it wasn't a trick, it was the field; but the farmer couldn't be trusted; that much he did know.

"A bad dream," he said, screwing his eyes shut. "It's just a bad dream."

Calham smiled to himself and stood up. He slid his chair back under the table and headed out of the kitchen with his mug still in his hand. He lingered in the doorway to the hall and looked back at Matt.

Matt opened his eyes again to find the figment of his waking nightmare still in front of him and still all too real. He sighed with open disappointment.

"So what happens now?"

"Now?" said Calham. "We wait."

Calham winked at him and disappeared behind a door in the gloomy hall beyond the kitchen.

* * *

The sun set on Shadowbrook Farm, casting long shadows across the surrounding fields that spread and joined to usher in the waiting darkness. A cold, meager light flickered from one of the ground floor windows of the farmhouse. Inside, canned laughter blurted out through the open lounge door and along the hallway to the kitchen, as the ghostly blue reflections of an unseen television set played over the hall wall. Matt woke with a start and looked around the kitchen in bewilderment, roused from his sleep by the noise. He wiped dribble from his mouth and yawned. Then he frowned as he noticed something shiny sat on the crammed shelves against the kitchen wall. He began to stare at it intently, even as specific memories of it evaded his conscious mind. The sound of television's canned laughter swelled as the lounge door opened all the way. Calham shuffled out into the hall, just as Matt dropped his head to his arms on the tabletop and pretended to be asleep. Calham entered the kitchen and peered at Matt for a moment. He then turned away and took a bottle of cheap whiskey and a glass from one of the cupboards. He then paused and stared at Matt again, for longer this time. He moved closer to the table and hovered there over his captive. He then slammed the glass down hard on its surface near to his face. Matt didn't flinch, though he pretended to stir in his sleep. Apparently satisfied by this, Calham picked up the whiskey glass and trudged back into the hall with it. His bulky silhouette paused there again and looked back at Matt one last time, before finally disappearing into the lounge, leaving the door ajar.

Matt carefully raised his head and checked to see if the coast was clear behind him. He then slowly rose as straight as his chains would allow, and stretched forwards to examine the shelf on the adjacent wall again. A child's mobile of carved, metal farmyard animals, tangled in wires, sat scrunched up on the shelf next to a collection of unevenly arranged books and tins. Matt leaned further over the table to get a better look at this object that teased his forgotten memories, but his chain pulled taught against the table. Matt cursed silently and stared anxiously at the lounge door in the hallway, ready for it to whip open at any minute. His chest rose and fell rapidly, as he watched the door with anxious eyes.

Nothing.

Matt gently lowered himself back on to his seat. He rested his chin on to his folded arms to genuinely try for sleep again, though he didn't take his eyes off the tangled toy on the shelf.

* * *

A steaming cup of coffee thumped down on to the kitchen table next to Matt's face. His eyes snapped open and he raised his groggy features. Calham moved to the window and stooped to look out over the cornfields as he smoked a cigarette.

"Morning," he said. "These early starts taking it out of you?"

"No," said Matt. "Just the murders and magic."

Calham grinned, enjoying the banter. He pulled one last drag from his cigarette and blew smoke into the air before stubbing it out.

"I think you're going to change your opinion of me today," he said.

"It can't get any lower."

"We'll see," said the farmer.

CHAPTER SIXTEEN

Matt stood beneath the shower in a daze, letting the hot water massage his aching muscles. When he finally emerged from the downstairs bathroom with damp hair and a clean face, Calham was waiting for him, leaning idly against the hallway wall with the shotgun cradled in his arms. The farmer nodded at his captive with approval. The message was clear: compliance brought privileges. Matt wondered just how compliant he was expected to be.

Calham and Matt left the farmhouse under grey, foreboding skies and crossed over to the second barn where they'd left the hooded woman. Matt hesitated at the barn door, remembering the horrors that he'd seen inside. Calham chuckled to himself, relishing his fear.

"Go on," he said. "He's chained up. You don't bother him, and he won't eat you."

Matt reluctantly opened the barn door and stepped into the shadows inside. He stuck to the wall and felt his way forwards, swimming blindly through the darkness. He heard something in front of him, stirring and grunting. The sound of heavy chains dragged across the floor. He paused and looked back towards the light of the open door for reassurance. He saw Calham there behind him. The farmer nodded to him, and so he pushed on through the blackness, until he eventually felt a hand on his shoulder and stopped again. The overhead fluorescent strip lighting plinked and flickered into life, and Matt once again found himself in the crèche's straw-strewn bedding area. Matt stared down in disbelief at the bound woman lying on the straw in front of him, still naked apart from her hooded face.

It wasn't a dream after all.

Matt slowly shook his head at this long, sick joke still playing out in his head, trying to deny the sights his eyes were showing him, and the connotations of these sights that he dared not ponder. Calham appeared at his side, wearing a black ski mask and holding a small, black bottle in his hand. He handed Matt a second ski mask.

"Put it on," he said.

Matt looked at him gravely; what the hell now? He slowly pulled the mask over his pale features. Calham checked him and nodded his approval. He then approached the woman. Hearing his footfalls, she scrabbled back against the wall and tried to flatten herself into it, her hooded head jerking about trying to locate the farmer. Calham knelt down next to her, then turned to face Matt with dark delight.

"You ready?" he whispered.

Before Matt could respond, Calham whipped the hood off to reveal the startled woman's gagged features. Matt just stared at her. It really was the same woman he watched Calham abduct, torture and finally kill two days before. The same woman whose corpse he carried over the fallow field, and the same woman they buried in its foul soil. He wobbled and reached out for something to steady himself on, but failed and slipped down to the ground. Calham sniggered uncontrollably, as the miracle woman's eyes bulged with confusion and fear.

Matt started to pull his ski mask off to catch his breath. Calham stopped laughing and quickly positioned himself between Matt and the woman. He hurriedly tipped the dark bottle of chloroform out against a rag and then clamped it over the woman's mouth. Her eyelids fluttered in response and a moment later she flopped back against the straw bedding.

Matt sat there on the ground with his mask in his hands, his hair sticking up, taking deep, rapid breaths. Calham shook his head in disappointment, as he unfastened the leather restraints from the woman's wrists and ankles.

"Bloody stupid," he said. "What do you think the mask was for?"

"It's all real, isn't it?" said Matt.

"Of course it's real."

"How did you do it? I saw you kill her."

"I told you," said Calham. "It's the soil, there's something in it."

Matt threw his mask on the floor.

"Grab her clothes over there," said Calham. "We're not done yet."

Matt and Calham carried the woman's limp, dressed body out to the Land Rover and put her in the back. They then climbed in the front. Calham started up the engine and pulled away, cutting out over the cornfield, away from the farm.

The Land Rover left the farm track and picked up speed along the surrounding country lanes, as Matt, shackled in his seat, looked out over the passing green landscape and slowly began to remember the route. He turned to Calham as if to speak, but the other man kept his eyes fixed firmly on the road, all business. The Land Rover picked its way around more winding country lanes, as dark rain clouds began to gather on the horizon.

The Land Rover slowed as it approached the site of the woman's abduction at the bend in the road just two days before. It pulled off the lane just before the sharp bend hooked around a blind corner of undergrowth, right where Calham originally took the woman, and then disappeared into the cover of the adjacent woods. Matt looked out through the windscreen as the Land Rover drew to a halt next to the woman's abandoned, foliage-covered 4x4. He silently watched Calham climb out and clear away the camouflaging brush that covered it. Calham then returned to the rear of the Land Rover and carried the sleeping woman back over to her vehicle. He placed her inside and climbed in next to her. He reversed the 4X4, positioning it at the edge of the clearing next to the road. He then climbed out and pulled the woman across, putting her in the driver's seat. Matt watched him return to the Land Rover, beaming with the smug pride of a job well done. The farmer then unchained Matt and ushered him over to the 4x4 to inspect his handiwork.

"I don't understand," said Matt.

"She'll wake up next to the road and assume she pulled over for a rest and fell asleep," said Calham. "The missing couple of days will be a mystery, but then life's full of mysteries."

Matt felt something powerful, imminent suddenly welling up inside him. It was more than just memories returning to him, it was knowledge, it was truth; truth that had been earned through the hardest of yards.

"She'll remember," he said.

"They never remember," said Calham.

"I did."

Matt pondered his own response for a moment, not fully comprehending the words or how they had found their way into his mouth. But the moment the words were said, he knew he was telling the truth. He'd been here before.

"You're special," said the farmer.

It then hit Matt like a train.

His mind raced with fleeting fragments of memories: wandering the field through the early morning mist; driving through the country following a cold, vague trail of faded memories; finding his car secreted in the clearing; picking a route through the dark woods and cutting across the swaying field of corn; the bleak view of Shadowbrook Farm for the "first time"; meeting Calham outside the farmhouse, Duke the border collie barking at him; eyeing Calham's cluttered kitchen as the farmer brewed tea; holding up the child's toy mobile of dangling animal shapes; Calham drawing the carving knife across his throat...

He remembered.

He coughed and doubled over feeling sick, wheezing, trying to snatch elusive breaths that his lungs refused to take down. He raised his deathly white features to Calham and swallowed hard.

"You did this to me," said Matt.

It was a statement, not a question.

"Yes," said Calham.

"Oh God," said Matt. "Oh God..."

"But you're different to all the rest..." said Calham. "...you always remember, eventually."

Matt stared at the farmer, trying to digest his words.

"Always?" said Matt.

"You must have found your way back to the farm nearly a dozen times now."

Matt's head began to spin faster and faster as it all soaked in. The image of the farmer danced and doubled as his vision shook apart. One Calham became two; two became four. He slumped to the ground.

"You could say we're...old friends."

Matt instinctively curled his body into a foetal shape, craving the long-lost safety of the womb. He started to convulse and shock took hold of him. His eyes rolled up into the back of his head and their lids fluttered uncontrollably. A welcome blackness welled up from somewhere in the depths of his of mind and quickly spread to consume him. He began to feel himself falling.

CHAPTER SEVENTEEN

Matt awoke to find he was chained to his chair and slumped face-first across the kitchen table in the farmhouse. It was night, but the light was on above him. He raised his head and stared into space, no longer sure of anything in his own lapsed sense of chronology and reality. His face was pale and covered in a sickly sheen of sweat, as if he'd been fighting through a ravenous fever while asleep.

The kitchen door swung open silently to reveal Calham. The farmer had the tell-tale glazed eyes of someone who had been drinking heavily. He hung back for a moment and observed Matt suspiciously. Finally he sighed and pulled his jacket off, and moved towards to the kitchen cupboards. He reached up and took out a bottle of cheap Scotch and two glasses, then sat down opposite Matt. He poured out two generous measures and slid one of the glasses towards Matt.

"Go on," he said. "It's medicinal."

Matt hesitated, then took a sip.

"How long have you been doing this to me?" said Matt.

The farmer thought carefully before answering.

"I suppose our little game's been going on for just over a year now."

Matt tasted the whiskey again; its strength and warmth seemed to be bringing him back round.

"In the beginning," he said. "Was it like the woman? An ambush?"

Calham nodded.

"I've got a lot of routes and sweet-spots I like to use," said the farmer. "It's a wild and empty country for those on the back roads."

"I had nightmares. I was being being buried under the earth and screaming," said Matt. "I was alive, and I couldn't get out."

Matt looked Calham in the eye.

"You're wrong," he said. "They do remember."

"You're the only one that's ever found his way back to the farm," said Calham.

The farmer necked his whiskey and chuckled to himself wryly as he refilled his glass.

"And believe me, there's been enough of them over the years."

Calham winked at Matt, genuinely thinking he might find the comment funny. Matt took a nervous gulp of his own drink, wondering just how many there had been. He watched Calham take out his cigarettes and light up.

"Got a spare one of those?" he said.

Calham raised an eyebrow, before offering the pack to Matt and lighting him. Matt took a long, deep drag and leaned back, blowing the smoke out with a sigh. He tried to forget his situation for a moment; the ever-present chains that bound him, the shotgun in the other room, the twisted thing lurking in the shed. If he held his nerve, this might be his chance to finally have some straight answers from his captor. He looked Calham directly in the eye again.

"Why do you do it?" he asked.

"What?" said Calham. "Kill them, or bring them back?"

"Both," said Matt.

Calham smoked and pondered the question for a moment; something he'd never asked himself; but then why would he, when the answer was so simple, so obvious. He leaned forwards, deliberately invading Matt's space, captivated by the intimacy of both the question and the prospect of confessing his secrets.

"I kill them because I love it," he whispered. "I fucking love it...and because I can."

Calham leaned back again, enjoying the satisfaction of telling another soul the simple truth behind his atrocities and disturbing them at the same time. His eyes gleamed with pleasure as he spoke again.

"I bring them back because that's the way it's supposed to be," he said. "The field's there for a purpose. And so am I."

Matt gazed at him, horrified. Then something else began to rise within him and his stare hardened.

"Convenient," he said, still holding his captor's gaze.

"What?" said Calham.

"Convenient," he repeated . "No guilt. Victims that don't stay dead. So hey, what's the problem? You don't carry one ounce of remorse for what you've done to those people. For what you've done to me."

Calham shrugged and leaned back, his blunted emotions genuinely perplexed by the suggestion.

"I take what I need, and then I put back in the ground what's left," said the farmer. "It all comes around. It all balances out in the end."

"Just like nature," suggested Matt.

"Exactly," said Calham.

The farmer drained his glass and topped it up with more whiskey, only he didn't seem to be enjoying the taste anymore.

"Just two horrific days out of your life that you won't remember," said Matt. "Then on the third day everything's back to normal."

"Yeah," said Calham. "Now you're getting it,"

Matt laughed and shook his head. He straightened up against his captor's confused gaze.

"You really are a piece of work," he said. "So why me? Why show me all this? What you do, how you go about your...business."

"I told you," said Calham. "You're the one that always remembers. You're the one that turns up here each time looking for answers."

"Yeah," said Matt. "But why show me? What makes you think I need to see this gristly shit? Why would I want to learn exactly what you've put me through time and time again? Is that part of the kick too?"

Calham struggled to find the words to form a reply; the burly farmer had suddenly lost all of his usual bravado.

"There's no one else," he said. "I've never had anyone to tell before."

Calham leaned closer, his face reddening.

"You keep turning up like a bad penny, and we play cat and mouse," he said. "I try and guess how much you've remembered this time around, and you try and work out what happened to you."

The farmer stared at the floor for a few moments, before daring to make eye contact again.

"Believe it or not," he said. "You're the closest thing I've got to a friend."

The two men sat in awkward silence, avoiding each other's gaze for what seemed like an eternity.

"You going to say something then?" said Calham.

"It should be funny," said Matt. "Somehow, you've stumbled across the secret to eternal life, and you've used it as an excuse to kill. You've perverted something beautiful into a tool for getting off on your sick little murder fantasies."

Calham shifted around in his seat uncomfortably, wounded by the words, making him feel ugly and defensive.

"I know I'm ill," said Calham. "But that's not the point..."

"You're not ill," said Matt. "You're a fucking lunatic!"

In one swift movement, Calham pulled a small blade from his boot and stabbed it down hard into Matt's right hand, staking it to the tabletop. Matt howled with pain and pulled vainly at the knife's handle. Calham was on him in seconds, his large hand around Matt's throat. He pushed his manic face into Matt's and snarled.

"Why did I show you all this?" he said. "Because this time, when I kill you, it'll be the last time. No more coming back, no more memories. This time, you stay in the ground for good."

Calham jumped up from the table, grabbing the whiskey bottle and his jacket, and marching out, slamming the door behind him. Matt slowly raised his eyes and dared to look at the knife pinning his hand to the table. He groaned at the sight and felt waves of thick nausea slide over him. Through the kitchen window he could see the Land Rover's headlights flick on, illuminating the fallow field outside. Moments later its engine rumbled into life and revved angrily, before roaring away across the cornfields and off into the darkness.

CHAPTER EIGHTEEN

Matt heard the Land Rover's straining engine fade with its departure into the night. He quickly scanned the kitchen for something close by with which to pick the lock on his chains. Once again, his eyes found the toy mobile of metal animal shapes hanging from the shelf in the corner. He looked down at the knife through his hand where it was staked to the table. He grabbed the knife's handle and pulled at it. It didn't budge. He tried again, harder this time, grunting with effort, and felt it began to loosen, bringing bright, fresh, startling pain to the wound there. He did his best to shut the pain down in his mind, worried it might make him pass out and quickly mustered a third attempt. He strained with effort, as he pulled at the knife, until finally it popped free of his punctured hand. He leaned back in his chair and sighed with relief; his red face covered in sweat. He then bent down to look under the table at the taught length of chain still tethering his waist to one of its thick oak legs. Fuelled by the possibility of escape, Matt stood and gripped the kitchen table with both hands. He heaved at it, dragging it towards the shelf where the mobile lay. The weight was too much for him though and he had to keep stopping and starting. The heavy oak table gradually moved inch by frustrating inch, as Matt trembled with effort and scraped it slowly across the tiles towards the shelves in the corner. Moaning through gritted teeth, he finally succeeded in pulling the table close enough to the wall to be within reaching distance of the mobile. He allowed himself a moment of respite, then gathered his strength again and stretched to reach for the mobile. After several failed attempts his fingertips snagged one of the dangling figures and he jerked down on it, snapping the wire in the process. He looked down at the shape that had broken free in his hand and his lips pursed into a humourless smirk. Out of the plethora of farm animals hanging from the mobile, he'd snagged a crude carving of the farmer himself: a sheet metal outline of him taking aim with his shotgun. He supposed the homemade mobile served as childlike reflection of this forgotten place and perfectly summed up the hierarchy of Calham's private crumbling universe. A variety of livestock living under one crazed master who ruled with violence. Only these days there were no more dumb animals left to lord over at Shadowbrook Farm; just Duke, Henry and a transient succession of unfortunate motorists, himself included.

 Matt took the farmer shape and plugged the shotgun-shaped sliver of metal into the padlock chained around his waist. He wiggled and angled the piece of metal around the lock, trying to pick it, more through luck rather than judgment.

 Unfortunately, his run of bad luck seemed to be holding.

* * *

The cornfields surrounding Shadowbrook Farm swayed and danced in the breeze beneath a fat, silvery full moon. Clouds drew a temporary veil across the moonlight and the shadows of the nearby woods reached towards the farm with long withered fingers.

All was quiet, except for the lazy rustle of the corn on the wind.

Then the sound of an engine.

Getting closer.

In the distance, headlights swept through the woods, illuminating the gnarly, ancient trees there. The Land Rover's lights then swung about and headed straight for Shadowbrook Farm.

* * *

Matt was still lost in deep concentration, focused on working the lock, when he heard the Land Rover approaching. He felt his stomach knot and tighten. Surely the farmer wasn't back already? He remained still for an age, listening to the droning engine draw nearer and nearer, refusing to believe his ears, just staring out through the window into the darkness with a blank expression of shock.

Eventually he began to look around the kitchen with dumbfounded haste. There was no way he'd pick the lock in time, and he'd dragged the table over to the other side of the room. He tried not to imagine what the farmer would do to him if he caught him trying to escape. Matt quickly pocketed his improvised lock-pick and grabbed the edge of the table to try and drag it back to its original position before the farmer returned. He strained and pulled, but again made slow progress with the heavy table. After long, agonizing bouts of effort for short gains, he froze again, as the Land Rover's beams swept over the kitchen, throwing shadows across his desperate features. Matt stared out through the window and into the headlights like the proverbial caught bunny, until the Land Rover's engine died and the lights faded. Matt gripped the table one last time and tried to haul it back to its original position. He dragged the legs ever-so-slowly across the kitchen floor, leaving a telltale trail of scuff marks on the tiles, until the table was finally back where it should be. He quickly pulled his chair back in against the table and sat down again, as he heard the burly farmer's footsteps approaching outside the door.

Then Matt looked down at his bloodied free hand. At the knife.
There was no time.
No other way.

Matt rolled his eyes and cursed his luck beneath his breath, as the footsteps drew nearer. He reluctantly flattened his bleeding palm against the table and raised the knife over it. The blade hovered over his outstretched hand as he hesitated, leaving the tip of the blade poised over his existing wound. Matt then closed his eyes and thumped the knife down as hard as he could, into both his hand and the table.

The kitchen door banged open behind him, revealing Calham's ruddy, drunken face. He stood in the doorway for a moment, swaying back and forth, glaring at Matt. Then the big man made straight for him. He snatched up the replanted knife in one swift movement, making Matt flinch and whine through gritted teeth. Calham then yanked Matt back by his collar, unlocked the padlock and began unwinding the chain from around his waist. He pulled the younger man to his feet.

"C'mon," said the farmer. "It's time."

Matt reeled from Calham's boozy breath and saw the glassy, faraway look in his eyes. He couldn't help but snatch another glimpse of the mobile's twirling metal shapes hanging from the shelf over the farmer's shoulder. Calham caught the look and pushed his knife up against Matt's throat.

"I said it's time."

Calham forced Matt out through the kitchen door by the scruff of his neck and into the darkness waiting beyond.

CHAPTER NINETEEN

Calham marched Matt towards the barns. Matt dragged his feet and cradled his injured hand, dread building inside him as he approached the workshop. Calham shoved him forwards into the light which was already spilling from the open doorway. Matt warily entered and reluctantly approached the area partitioned from the rest of the interior with haystacks; the area where Calham liked to play. The strip lighting overhead twitched on and off, making the workshop flicker. As he drew closer, Matt caught a glimpse of something strapped down against the surface of the workbench. He stopped and swallowed. Not again. There was a large hand at his back, and he felt himself being pushed forwards, into the farmer's makeshift torture cell. He made eye contact with a battered and bruised stranger in a torn suit bound to the workbench. The man stirred when he saw Matt and tried to rise, but was held fast by leather straps against the woodwork. He turned his swollen, marked face to track Matt as he approached. Then his imploring eyes grew wide with recognition and fear when he saw Calham enter the workshop carrying his shotgun. The man instinctively rocked and struggled against his restraints, but he was bound too tightly to escape. Calham ignored the man's writhing and faced Matt, looking him in the eye. The drunken farmer bobbed around unsteadily in front of him, trying to settle into an elusive centre of gravity. Calham produced the knife that he'd already used on Matt's hand, but this time he turned it around and offered it to him handle-first. Matt stared at the knife and then at the shotgun resting at Calham's side. The farmer watched him closely with glazed eyes.

"This is why I showed you," said Calham.

He drove the knife's blade down hard into the workbench with a thud. He took a step back and continued to eye Matt, waiting for his response.

There was none.

"Take it," said Calham.

Matt remained perfectly still.

"You don't understand it..." said Calham. "...because you haven't tasted it."

Matt stared at the knife with naked contempt.

"I meant what I said," said Calham. "If you're not with me, you're going in the ground for good this time."

Matt slowly reached for the knife. His hand hovered over the handle. The man on the workbench began to moan and shake his head.

"Just try it," said Calham. "We can bring him back later."

Matt looked at his supposed victim, and then back at Calham.

"Do it."

Matt lowered his gaze and eyed the blood dripping from his own wounded hand as it hovered over the knife. He quickly withdrew the hand and took a step back from the restrained man, as if suddenly finding himself too close to the edge of some great, black abyss.

"No," said Matt. "I don't want to play God."

Calham stared into Matt for a long time with cold, hurt, watery eyes. His expression was that of a spurned lover wrestling with the rage and despair of rejection. He took a deep breath and stepped forward to retrieve the knife. His face began to burn with embarrassment, as the other two men watched nervously and awaited his reaction. Despite this, Calham still held Matt's gaze, hoping the younger man might yet change his mind. Eventually though, cold resignation settled into the farmer's features, and they hardened as he finally accepted defeat.

"Could've worked..." he said to himself.

Calham jabbed the shotgun forwards, smashing the stock into Matt's face. A huge gaping maw of blackness instantly opened wide and swallowed Matt whole.

Once again, he felt himself falling.

CHAPTER TWENTY

Matt awoke to find himself on the ground and once again shackled to the tethering ring at the foot of the barn's workbench. He stood with some difficulty, swaying groggily, and touched a fresh, purpling bruise that was swelling on his face.

"I thought he'd killed you."

Matt looked up at the stranger chained against the workbench.

The stranger that he was supposed to torture and kill.

"Oh, he has," said Matt. "You OK?"

"I think so," said the man. "What's your name?"

"Matt," he said.

"Rob," said the other man.

Matt nodded at him and steadied himself against the bench, as a rush of dizziness swirled up inside and pulled at his stomach and head.

"How much slack have you got on that chain, Matt?"

Matt held up his hands and pulled the chain taught against his chest. Rob frowned through his own bruising.

"Is there anything around you?" said Rob. "On the floor? Something sharp maybe?"

Matt slowly rotated, his eyes searching the floor, but he was still dazed and shuffled like a tired toddler. He looked back at Rob blankly and shook his head.

"OK," said Rob. "OK, let's think for a minute."

A thought fired in Matt's fogged brain. He snorted and dug his hand into one of the pockets of his overalls and slowly retrieved the metal shape he'd stolen from the child's mobile; the crude rendering of the homicidal farmer whose strange world had collided so violently with theirs. Matt held up the carving for Rob to see. A sly grin broke across his face.

"I know we've only just met," said Rob. "But I think I love you."

Matt turned the piece of metal awkwardly using both hands and pushed it into the padlock that secured the chain around his wrists. He went to work picking the lock, trying to ignore the sharp pain flaring through his hand where Calham had driven his knife clean through. As he fiddled with the lock the wound worked itself open and began to bleed again.

"I've tried this before," said Matt. "It's not easy."

"Don't worry," said Rob. "You'll get it."

Matt worked at the lock, but lost his grip on the metal figure and watched it drop to the floor. He let out a flustered sigh, picked it and started again. Rob watched his progress nervously.

"How long's he had you here?" he said.

Matt continued to concentrate on the padlock, answering Rob without really considering his reply.

"A couple of days."

"You're still in pretty good shape," said Rob. "He must like you."

"I don't think he likes anyone," said Matt. "Except maybe Henry."

"Who's Henry?"

Matt paused for a moment and looked Rob in the eye.

"You don't want to know."

Matt went back to work on the lock, as worry began to pull at the lines on Rob's battered face. The other man wet his dry lips and started to talk quickly, as if the sound of his own voice might somehow stave off the fear that was swelling inside.

"I was driving back from an interview today," he said. "I've been trying to move back to this part of the world for ages now, buy a house here, but it's difficult, you know? You get used to the salaries in London and then everywhere else, everywhere else is..."

Matt screwed his face tight as he struggled to tease the lock, gently steering the metal and trying to sense the intricate pressure points within.

"Go on," he said.

"It was great," said Rob. "The job sounded great, they liked me, I know people they know. They asked me to stay on and they took me out to dinner. Oh yeah, I thought, I'm in, I've got it."

"Good for you."

"Called my girlfriend," he continued. "Told her I'd be a little late. Couple of drinks with my new colleagues..."

Rob forced out a hollow chuckle.

"...couple of drinks too many. You try and cut cross country around here and all the roads look the bloody same. Especially after dark."

"Then this Land Rover's behind me, out of nowhere. Full beam, he's up my arse. I tried to let him pass, but he wouldn't."

Matt stopped again. Something wasn't right. He looked gravely at Rob .

"He ran you off the road?"

"Oh yeah," said Rob. "My Audi must look like a bloody horseshoe by now."

Matt swallowed dryly and redoubled his efforts on the lock. This was bad. He knew the significance of the statement, even if his new ally didn't. Calham didn't just run people off the road. He planned and took his victims carefully, and then returned them just as carefully too. If the farmer took Rob sloppily in the heat of the moment, it meant he had no intention of completing the cycle; no intention of letting the man survive to be returned to his old life. Or even worse, it meant he no longer cared what happened to himself, to Matt, to anyone.

He found himself breathing faster and rushing his attempts to pick the lock.

"I don't normally think of myself as a glass half empty type," said Rob. "But..."

"Why me?" said Matt.

"Yeah," said Rob. "Why me?"

Rob fell quiet and watched Matt's strained efforts with the lock in silence. The overhead fluorescent strip began to flutter on and off again, flickering the space between two men with alternating flashes of darkness and light. Matt frowned at the added distraction, but tried to keep his focus on the lock.

"I should be back home now," said Rob. "Surprising Ellen with the good news. She's wanted to get out of London for so long. I couldn't wait to see the look on her face..."

"*Can't* wait," said Matt. "You *can't* wait."

"Sure," said Rob. "Sure...she's a country girl, you know. Loves all that open space, the deafening silence, the smell of shit everywhere, the inbreeding...oh God I want to be back to London. They just mug you there."

"Hang on," said Matt. "We'll get you there. But I'm driving."

Matt grinned at Rob and the other man appeared to take some comfort from it. He managed a genuine smile back, as if he really believed Matt might somehow save them.

"You got a lady?" said Rob.

"Yeah," said Matt. "Sandra."

"What's she like?"

"Tough," said Matt. "Really tough. She's got me whipped, and I love it."

"She busts your balls, eh?"

Matt nodded as a wide, nostalgic smile played across his face. Then that smile began to decay, and his warmth cooled, as the lost memories of his infidelities seeped back into his exhausted mind. It was a wave of memories, bitter realities from his past forcing their way back into this new life, resurrecting his last moments with Sandra. Their forgotten break up hit him for the first time in this lifetime. Then his seemingly endless infidelities were right behind it. All this unwanted knowledge and guilt slid down over his chest like a thick hot tar, filling his lungs, squeezing his heart, suffocating him. What a prick he'd been. Maybe this farm, the field, was his fate for not just one badly lived life, but a whole series of lives wasted. A slew of repeated mistakes and bad calls that he never learned from, destructive behaviour to himself and those he professed to love that never changed no matter how many fresh chances he was given. Maybe he was right where he deserved to be after all.

He stared at the floor as the crushing weight of these memories and what they all added up to finally took hold. He was not the man he thought hc was. He'd repeatedly proven himself capable of being much, much worse. He continued to absently play the padlock, as he cursed himself for his past actions, momentarily unaware that the mechanism had sprung open in his hands.

"You did it," said Rob. "You fucking did it."

Matt looked down in surprise at the open padlock and the slack chains sliding from his wrists. He'd begun to imagine he'd always be chained in this life, but fate again seemed to have other plans for him.

"Come on," said Rob, rocking excitedly against his restraints. "Let's go."

Matt watched his chains unravel and run, sliding to the floor. He slowly pulled apart his free hands and stared at them, turning the palms up, finally registering his escape.

"They're beautiful," said Rob. "Now let's move."

CHAPTER TWENTY-ONE

The door to the workshop barn slowly creaked open and Matt peered out into the darkness beyond. He held a shining cleaver in his hand from the workshop. He scanned the gloom, letting his eyes adjust to it, gradually registering the vague outlines of the farmhouse and barns, and the rustling, moonlit cornfields that surrounded it, as he searched the shadows for signs of the farmer.

Nothing.

Matt stepped out into the night and beckoned for Rob to join him. They both stared with wide eyes at the black silhouette of the farmhouse. The lights were off and there was no sign of life within. Matt tried to hand the cleaver to Rob, but the other man wouldn't touch it. Matt tiptoed over to the nearby Land Rover, constantly looking this way and that. He gently squeezed the driver's side handle until it popped free and pulled the vehicle's door open very, very slowly. Matt held his breath as a small, oily squeak escaped the metal hinges. His eyes instinctively darted back to the farmhouse, his heart rising to his mouth, but still there was no sign of any reaction there. He carefully swung the door the rest of the way open and leaned in across the seat. He checked the dashboard and the glove compartment, but there was no sign of the keys.

Matt turned to Rob and shook his head. He gently pushed the Land Rover door closed again and crept back over to his fellow escapee. He pointed the cleaver towards the farmhouse.

"I'm going to try for the keys." he whispered.

Rob grabbed Matt's arm and shook his head. His eyes were urgent, almost bulging out of his head with panic.

"No..."

"Just keep lookout," said Matt.

Matt turned away before Rob could protest again and quietly approached the foreboding silhouette of the farmhouse. As he drew nearer, he peered in through the kitchen window at the moonlit interior, but could see little more than shadows there. He crept up to the front door and flattened himself against the wall there. He closed his eyes and took a deep breath in an attempt to slow his racing heart. He then slowly lifted the latch on the door and gently edged it open.

* * *

Matt stepped into a kitchen full of unfamiliar shadows and lingered in the doorway, waiting for his eyes to adjust to the gloom again. A low, steady growl rose out of the darkness up ahead. Matt could make out two fierce eyes shining there in the blackness. He took a step forwards. The growling became louder.

"Shhhh Duke," whispered Matt. "Good boy."

The growling persisted like a held note and continued to rise. Matt took another step. And another. The dog's outline became more distinct to him as he moved closer.

"Gooood Duke," said Matt. "Gooood boy."

Matt squatted down next to the angry dog and offered it an upturned hand. The dog's mouth pulled back into a snarl as it prepared to bite. Matt brought the cleaver down hard with his other hand straight on to the back of Duke's neck. The animal spasmed and yelped. Matt instantly struck again without thinking, and the dog was dead. He pulled the cleaver from the dog's sticky, matted coat.

"Stay," he said.

Matt looked up at the ceiling and waited for the sound of heavy footsteps, but none came. He stood and faced the hall door. He raised the bloodied cleaver again, ready to deliver another blow to anyone waiting behind it in ambush and snatched the door open.

The hall was empty.

Matt tiptoed into the hall and found himself staring at the closed lounge door. He moved in closer and gently pushed it open. The drab room was empty, only occupied by a TV, furniture and shadows, much to his relief. He felt his way around the lounge in the moonlight, checking the coffee table, shelves and other surfaces for the Land Rover's keys.

Nothing.

He returned to the hall and quietly followed it to the foot of the staircase. His eyes tracked the gradually darkening steps upwards until they disappeared completely, swallowed by a sea of blackness at the top. He took the first step, then hesitated, as his guts turned and knotted in his belly in protest.

* * *

Rob shivered as he waited out in the cold night air, caught in the open between the farmhouse and its outbuildings, and between his urge to escape and a sense of loyalty to the man who had just released him. His eyes darted from one distant, dark swaying patch of corn to the next, as he tried not to imagine the worst. He slowly turned his head, catching a faint sound on the wind. He looked back towards the barns.

A scratching noise.

Rob turned through three hundred and sixty degrees and checked around in the darkness. Were there other prisoners still inside? They'd been so focused on their own escape; they never entertained the possibility that there may be others chained up too. He braced himself and followed the scratching noise to the furthest barn.

* * *

Matt slowly crept up the farmhouse stairs, his muscles tensed, and his eyes strained wide to search the waiting shadows. Every inch of him was on edge, prepared for an attack. He was halfway up the stairs when one of the treads gave slightly under his weight and let out a loud creak.

Matt froze. He silently cursed his clumsiness and waited for the inevitable reaction from somewhere in the blackness at the top of the stairs.

Again, there was nothing.

Matt gripped the banister and gently lifted his foot off the offending step. To his relief it issued only a slight creak this time. He took the rest of the steps more lightly and soon found himself face-to-face with three closed doors at the top of the upstairs landing.

He slowly reached out for the first door's handle and carefully turned it. He gently pushed open the bedroom door and peered around its edge. His eyes focused first on an old double bed lying in the centre of the room. A hulking shape was bunched under the covers there, but it was too dark for him to see a face. He forced himself to take a step closer. Then another. Soon enough he could make out Calham's gruff, sleeping features half-buried in the shadows. He watched his adversary closely, expecting him to suddenly jump up and attack; but no such ambush came. He continued to stare at the older man, fascinated by the thought that his tormentor, his killer, finally lay there before him, completely vulnerable. The thought of murder rose within him, and he instinctively gripped the cleaver in his hand. It would be easy in theory, but he wasn't that man. For all the bad things he'd done in his life, his lives, he wasn't a killer. Not when such an act could easily be avoided. He managed to peel his eyes away from the sleeping farmer and forced himself check the rest of the room for the keys.

Then he saw the wall. His jaw dropped and hung slack, forcing his mouth open in surprise, as he stared at the pattern on the wallpaper at the back of the room. The gloomy interior of the bedroom, was in fact, not decorated with tasteless wallpaper, as he'd first assumed. Now in the moonlight, he could clearly see that the walls were covered with hundreds of Polaroid photos. He edged closer to the wall for a better look. All of the photos showed the farmer's reborn victims, naked and tethered amongst the straw bedding area of the crèche barn.

His eyes drifted over dozens of pictures of disoriented victims flinching from the camera's flash, until they reached a bare patch of wall. He leaned in closer to examine the last few photographs leading up to this spot, dread thickening in his gut.

Sure enough, the last photo there was of a dazed-looking Matt, taken just a few days ago. His eyes were closed, and his face turned away from the glare of the camera's flash. Matt touched the picture with his fingertips and then leaned his whole hand against the wall for support, as a wave of nausea hit him. Trophies. Killers like this loved their trophies didn't they. And here was Calham's. His scrapbook laid open as evidence of the unbelievable. Even though he knew the truth, begin confronted with snapshots of his own demise and return was almost too much for his mind to take. He turned away from the pictures and approached the bed again. He looked down at Calham's ruddy, smug, contented, sleeping face, at his chest rising and falling, and slowly raised the cleaver, preparing to swing it at the monster's head. But something deep down, some remaining sense of right, wouldn't let him. This was what the farmer had wanted all along, wasn't it? For him to join Calham in his twisted games, to murder and resurrect. For the two to share the pleasures of predation and the cleansing absolution of the field. Killing the man would mean he'd won after all. He would become the monster too. He began to tremble. The cleaver shook in his hand. He tried to swing again, but still hesitated.

Then the moment was lost.

Matt lowered the weapon to his side, unable to do it.

* * *

Rob drew closer to the end barn.

The crèche.

The scratching sound was louder here. He leaned in against the barn door and put his ear next to the wood. He heard the scratching again, very clearly coming from inside. He also heard the sound of chain links being uncurled and dragged through the dirt. He was right. Someone else was chained up inside. He lifted the latch and slowly pulled the barn door open. He tried to peer inside, but this part of the barn was still pitch black.

"Hello?" he whispered. "Hello? It's OK, I'm here to help."

Something stirred ahead of him.

* * *

Matt steadied himself. He felt spent after his inner struggle and eventual failure to take Calham's life. The adrenalin of their escape now eluded him, and he was suddenly exhausted. He crossed over to an old dresser on the other side of the bedroom and checked its surface, rooting through combs, cotton reels, reading glasses and other tat.

But there were no car keys.

He eased out the top drawer to reveal bundles of socks and underwear stuffed inside. He gently slid out the second drawer too; more clothes. As he leaned down to pull out the third drawer, Calham's dead eyes opened and looked at him, reflected in the dresser's mirror. The farmer watched Matt from his bed with a stony expression .

Matt straightened up, clutching a set of car keys. He ran his thumb across the casing of the car key insignia, revealing a Mazda symbol. He quickly pocketed the keys and scanned the room again, still searching for the keys to the much closer Land Rover. He noticed a pair of trousers hanging from the bedpost. He glanced over at Calham's solemn, sleeping face, then cautiously approached him again. Matt stooped at the foot of the bed and dug his hands into the pockets of the trousers hanging there. As he searched, he didn't notice the shotgun silently being raised and brought to bear on him from the other end of the bed. Matt grinned to himself in the darkness and fished out the Land Rover's keys. It was then that he caught sight of Calham's cold, grey eyes boring into him. He dropped the keys and dived to the floor as the shotgun went off with a boom.

* * *

Rob took another step into the darkness of the crèche barn and blindly felt his way forward with outstretched hands.

"Hello? Are you there?"

He flinched at the loud blast outside, as Calham's shotgun discharged over at the farmhouse. He quickly turned and looked back at the open barn door behind him, his heart racing.

Another blast went off.

Rob remained there, half turned and rooted to the spot, unable to take his eyes off the open door. His head was flooded with panic, his body seized.

It was then that Henry attacked. Henry's hulking, twisted silhouette roared and launched itself out of the shadows ahead of Rob. Rob turned to face the creature and stumbled backwards, as a claw-like hand swiped at his chest. He scrambled backwards and fell out through the barn doorway and on to the ground outside. He stared up at the opening, his chest heaving, expecting Henry's misshapen figure to emerge from the blackness within; but the creature didn't follow. Rob instead caught a glimpse of something moving in his peripheral vision and turned in time to see the upstairs lights of the farmhouse flick on. Moments later the farmhouse's kitchen door banged open and Matt rushed out like a madman, sprinting across the farmyard towards the cornfields.

Rob scrambled to his feet, checked the crèche doorway one last time, and began running towards Matt.

"Wait!" he shouted. "Wait for me!"

Matt and Rob quickly cut out across the farm and met up ahead of the sea of swaying corn.

"You're not going to believe what I just bloody saw," said Rob.

"I think there's still a car in the woods," said Matt. "Past these fields."

"You think?" said Rob.

His eyes were like saucers, his heart was racing.

"I'm pretty sure," said Matt. "I've got the keys."

"Good enough," said Rob. "I've seen enough creepy shit tonight. Lead on."

Both men turned together, as the farmhouse door banged shut behind them. They saw Calham striding out towards the barn carrying his shotgun. The farmer moved steadily, confidently, and didn't appear to be in a rush, which was even more unnerving to the two men. Matt and Rob exchanged a nervous glance and quickly turned back to face the dense veil of corn swaying in front of them.

CHAPTER TWENTY-TWO

Matt pulled apart the tall stalks blocking his way and stepped into the jungle of corn. Rob followed him in, and the two men pushed forwards through the sea of swaying crops, unable to see more than a few feet ahead. A few seconds later both men froze. In the distance behind them they heard a loud, idiot whooping call from out of the darkness. It was a demented string of loud, but nonsensical, slurred words rising and falling. The effect was disturbing, like some feral animal imitating a small child's gibberish. Matt and Rob glanced at each other nervously, then pressed on again, moving faster than before.

* * *

Henry's hulking, deformed silhouette loped out of the shadows and emerged from the crèche barn's doorway. Calham trailed behind it, keeping a tight grip on the taught length of chain attached to Henry's collar. The beast paused and sniffed at the air excitedly like a rabid hound. It caught a scent and lunged forwards, jolting the farmer.

"That's it, Henry," said Calham. "Go get them."

Calham let go of the chain and watched Henry throw back its twisted foetus-like head and charge forwards into the night, flailing its powerful arms about wildly with manic delight. Henry bolted straight into the corn after Matt and Rob, flattening a wide path as it hunted its prey. Calham followed the creature's trail with measured strides, calmly reloading his shotgun as he walked. Up ahead, he could hear Henry crashing through the corn at speed, rasping and grunting like a wild animal.

* * *

Matt and Rob rushed ahead through the darkness now, all too aware of the beast at their heels, breathing hard, throwing themselves at the corn. Matt still took the lead, diving headlong into the stalks, with Rob constantly pushing at his back, urging him to move faster. So when Matt tripped and pitched forwards, Rob fell too, the two men colliding and becoming entangled in a heap on the ground.

"You OK?" said Matt.

"I think so..." said Rob. "...what?"

Matt held his finger up to his lips, requesting silence. Both men listened for a moment, their wide eyes scanning the curtain of corn surrounding them.

Nothing.

Just the sound of the wind pushing the swaying stalks back and forth.

"Do you think...?" Rob began.

It was then that Henry burst through the surrounding veil of corn and smashed into Rob flooring him. Matt was thrown backwards by the force of the attack too and hit the ground hard, momentarily dazed. Rob tried to scream as a gnarly, claw-like hand closed around his throat and hauled him high into the air. The beast shook him wildly, like a dog with a rabbit locked in its jaws. Rob's bulging eyes managed to focus on Matt, as his limp body danced through the air like a flailing puppet. Matt stared back in horror as his new friend was thrown this way and that by the brutish man-child. Then there was a sickening snap and Rob's head flopped loosely to one side. Henry continued to shake its victim furiously though, hardly noticing. Matt saw red. He shouted and lunged forwards, burying his cleaver deep into Henry's shoulder. The beast dropped Rob and threw its bulbous head back and howled in pain. Matt quickly snatched the cleaver back and struck again. This time it thudded into Henry's misshapen chest. Again, Matt pulled on the cleaver to retrieve it, but Henry began to thrash about wildly and it caught Matt with the back of a fist, batting him to the ground.

Matt let out a stifled yelp and glanced down at his leg. The cleaver's handle was still in his grip, but its blade was now protruding from his own thigh. He swallowed hard and blinked away tears of pain. Behind him, Henry was whimpering like some monstrous child. Matt gritted his teeth and pulled the cleaver out. He rolled his eyes and rode the spasms of resulting pain that shivered through his body.

When he looked up again, Henry had gone. The only sign of the creature was a splatter of its own blood next to Rob's crushed body. Matt stared at him. The dead man's eyes seemed stare back.

You said you'd save me. You said we were getting out of here together. You promised....

Matt forced himself to look away from Rob's inert face. He gripped his wounded thigh and limped off in the direction he'd been heading in before the fall. The forgotten cleaver lay behind in the flattened corn.

CHAPTER TWENTY-THREE

Matt fell out of the veil of swaying corn and stumbled towards the edge of the woods. He paused and looked back at the moonlit field, but he couldn't see any sign of his pursuers. He limped on through the woods, looking this way, then that, as he moved between the trees, struggling to follow a trail that was faint even in the daylight. He lurched on though, leaning on tree trunks for support, trying to orientate himself in the shadows. Eventually he emerged from the treeline and into a small clearing nestled in the woods. His breathing was hard and fast, and as the spent adrenalin began to ebb again from his exhausted body, he found himself barely able to remain on his feet, yet he still managed a smile when he saw his abandoned car and the rented Mazda up ahead. He thumped his fist against the nearest tree trunk and sighed under his breath.

"Yes," he whispered.

He pulled the Mazda's keys from his pocket and limped over to the car. He reached the driver's side and hurriedly tried the keys in the door, somehow expecting them not to fit; but he squeezed the handle and the door popped open. It was then that he heard a whimpering sound in the woods behind him. He whipped around and scanned the trees that surrounded the clearing. He could see nothing, yet the whimpering grew louder, as if moving closer. Then his wide eyes fixed on a large shadow on the trail between the trees, shuffling towards him.

Henry's twisted silhouette emerged from the woods. Its enormous head was bowed, and its pace was slow. It forlornly dragged its length of chain behind it like a lost and wounded dog trying to elicit sympathy. Matt tried to move, but he found himself frozen to the spot with fear. He watched as Henry made straight for him, shuffling closer and closer. The whimpering began to tail off, gradually lowering and flattening out into groaning sound. Then that groaning changed pitch again and slowly turned into a steadily rising growl of anger.

Matt carefully edged himself into the car, as Henry slowly raised its snarling, salivating features to focus on its prey. Matt fumbled with his key in the darkness, desperately trying to find the ignition, but still too scared to take his eyes off the advancing creature. After a few attempts, Matt managed to slot the key in. He tried to turn the engine over, but it merely strained and failed to catch. Henry growled in response and picked up the pace, raising its arms out from its sides as it approached the car, as if to cut off any chance of Matt escaping. Matt desperately turned the engine over again and again, but it still refused to start. A shadow fell over his moonlit features. He looked up through the windscreen to see Henry's hulking shape looming over the bonnet.

"Come on..." Matt shouted at the failing engine.

He turned the key in the ignition again, as Henry lashed out at him and smashed through the windscreen. Splinters of glass showered the car's interior, as the engine finally caught and roared into life. Matt put her in reverse and stamped on the accelerator pedal. The Mazda retreated at speed, and he watched his attacker diminish through what was left of the windscreen. Matt broke hard and jabbed the gear stick back into first, then floored it. He changed up to second and aimed the car straight at Henry as it began to screech at him. The Mazda ploughed into the beast with a wet thud and carried on for another twenty feet before crunching into a tree at the edge of the clearing.

Blackness.

Matt rolled his head and shook off his grogginess, as he slowly came round. He opened his eyes and found himself face to face with Henry's deformed features. The dead abomination was pinned against the tree, sprawled half over the car's bonnet and half through the broken windscreen. Matt edged away in disgust from the dead black eyes still staring at him out of the pulped foetus head hanging through the window. He tried the engine, but it wouldn't start. He continued to turn the key, unable to take his eyes off the misshapen face inches from his own. The engine wheezed, but still refused to catch. Matt was set to try the key a third time, when the twin barrels of Calham's shotgun slid gently out of the darkness towards the driver's side window and tapped against the glass.

"Get out," said Calham.

Matt turned and stared up at the dark figure at the side of the car. He screwed his eyes shut and silently cursed his luck. He slowly opened the door and eased himself out of the car, leaning back against the bodywork to avoid the shotgun's muzzle. Calham kept him covered as he examined Henry's mangled state. Matt watched the farmer lean in and gently stroke the beast's distorted features. Calham then snorted and turned, staring deep into Matt with cold, moist eyes. Matt didn't like that look one bit. He instinctively took a step back.

"Wait a minute, Calham..." he said.

"Look what you did."

There was no discernible emotion on the farmer's stony face, even though it was clear and bright in the moonlight. He had shut down. This was his game face, thought Matt. This was what it was like to stare into the face of someone holding a gun on you, not someone bluffing, but someone who was about to pull the trigger. Calham took a step closer to Matt and brought the shotgun level with his face.

"Calham," said Matt. "Please, don't..."

Calham squeezed the trigger, then eased off again at the last moment. He lowered the shotgun.

"Come on," said the farmer. "We don't have long."

CHAPTER TWENTY-FOUR

Matt and Calham rode in the Land Rover as it bounced along a dirt track in the darkness. The two men sat in silence, as the cab bumped and jolted over the rough ground between the cornfield and the woods. Matt's expression was one of defeat and resignation, while Calham's grim features were set with a stony resolve. The Land Rover halted, its brake lights burning against the clearing where Matt's smashed Mazda had pinned Henry to a tree, bleeding a red haze into the shadows of the surrounding woods. Calham climbed from the vehicle and marched Matt back over to the wrecked Mazda at gunpoint. He kept the shotgun and his hooded eyes trained on Matt, as the younger man climbed into the driver's side of the Mazda. Calham then slid in next to him. Matt tried to lean back in the driver's seat, keeping as far away as possible from Henry's grotesque corpse that was protruding through the smashed windscreen. Calham nodded a silent order to him, and Matt obediently tried the ignition key. The Mazda's engine strained, but failed to catch. He tried again.

Nothing.

"Again," said Calham.

Matt kept at the engine until it eventually rumbled back into life. Calham raised the shotgun to Matt's head and braced its stock into his shoulder.

"Slow," he said.

The mangled Mazda slowly reversed, releasing Henry's crushed corpse. The misshapen body gradually peeled away from the impacted tree trunk and flopped to the ground. The two men climbed out and approached it. Matt was nervy, hesitant, as if the squashed thing lying in the grass might somehow still be alive.

"Come on," said Calham. "He hasn't got long."

Matt stared in disbelief at Calham's suggestion until the farmer brought the shotgun to bear on him again. He reluctantly took hold of Henry's ragged corpse by its clawed hands and dragged it towards the back of the Land Rover.

The two men sat in silence again as the Land Rover trundled back towards the farmhouse through the dark. Matt stared at the hulking, broken body lying in the back, reflected in the rear-view mirror, and once again knew this was not the end of it. This was a nightmare that kept on giving, again and again, for him, and for the thing called Henry.

The Land Rover pulled up next to the edge of the fallow field. Calham cut the engine, but left the headlights on so that they illuminated the unholy ground that lay ahead. He unchained Matt and guided him to the back of the Land Rover. He took out a shovel and pointed it at Henry's body, his eyes still on Matt.

"Leave it," said Matt. "Let it rest."

Calham jabbed the shovel's handle into Matt's belly, making the younger man groan and double up.

"We're late," said Calham.

Matt straightened up and begrudgingly took hold of the corpse and began to pull it from the Land Rover. Calham drove the shovel into the earth a few feet away and left it sticking out at an angle, like a crooked cross in a cemetery. Matt struggled to drag

Henry's dead weight out into the area lit by the Land Rover's beams. Exhausted, he dumped the body down next to the shovel and took the handle. He then waited, listening to the quiet darkness, thinking, remembering. This was wrong. The creature had already turned and spoiled once. What would another resurrection do to it?

He turned to face Calham.

"This thing was warped the first time around," said Matt. "It's not going to get any better if you bring it back again. Just let it be."

"The only reason you're still breathing," said Calham. "Is because you can handle a shovel. So dig."

Calham stared at Matt with dead eyes. It wasn't just the booze; those eyes now seemed vacant of any humanity. Matt recognized that absence and bowed his head. He began to shovel the earth away. He was just so tired of it all. Calham lit a cigarette and took a drag, but he didn't like the taste. He made a face. It somehow tasted rotten now, just like everything else. He spat on the ground and rubbed his tongue over his teeth. The end of his cigarette glowed in the blackness, as he pulled on it again and pushed more smoke out into the night air. He spoke under his breath, almost reverentially.

"Poor, poor Henry," he said. "Don't worry, you'll soon be right as rain."

Matt toiled in the ancient earth, silhouetted in the Land Rover's headlights, as the farmer looked on and sighed a long, winding trail of smoke up into the night air. Matt dutifully excavated the fallow field's soil and then rolled Henry's corpse into the shallow grave without ceremony. He then filled the hole again and patted down the freshly turned earth when he was done. One down, one to go, he thought. The two men trudged wearily back towards the Land Rover.

Matt stopped.

"Why don't we dig Rob's now, while we're here?" he said.

Calham looked at Matt with genuine confusion, before he remembered his other prisoner.

* * *

Calham and Matt stood over Rob's dead body where it still lay in the flattened corn patch. Calham threw the spade to Matt, who caught it and shot back an angry look.

"Here?" he said. "What about the field?"

"We haven't got time," said Calham.

"You're going to leave him out here dead?"

Matt took a step forwards, his anger rising. Calham patted the stock of his shotgun as he cradled it in his arms and shook his head at the younger man.

"You're bringing that sorry animal back," said Matt. "But you're going to leave him out here dead?"

Calham nodded.

"Take him back up to the field," said Matt. "I'll bury him and then we can put him back where you found him."

"No," said Calham. "I took him in a rush. It's messy."

"You say they never remember, so where's the harm?"

"No," said Calham. "Just dig."

Matt stared at the ground, his mind turning too fast. He couldn't let this happen. He'd promised the man he'd get him out of this nightmare.

"You wanted someone to share this with..." he said. "...do this and I'll help you."

Calham moved closer to Matt and carefully looked him up and down.

"I made a mistake," he said slowly. "I thought you and me were getting along. I thought you were starting to understand. But how could you? You're just another piece of meat."

Matt stared at Calham.

Enough.

He threw the shovel down into the crushed corn stems next to Rob's lifeless body. Calham smiled to himself coldly and shook his head in mock disappointment. He jabbed the shotgun's stock into Matt's head, cracking it hard. Matt crumbled, unconscious before he hit the ground.

The farmer tutted to himself. He stood over Matt and pressed the muzzle of the shotgun into the back of Matt's head. He thumbed back the hammer and turned his face away in anticipation of the inevitable explosion of red when he pulled the trigger.

He waited.

The farmer sighed and eased the hammer back down. He placed the shotgun on the ground and picked up the shovel instead. He walked over to Rob's corpse and with cold detachment swung the shovel at the dead man's face three times, just to be sure. After all, things had a habit of not staying dead at Shadowbrook Farm. Calham snorted at his exertion and then drove the bloody spade down into the earth, pushing it in deeper with his boot. He began to steadily dig another grave there, amongst the corn.

CHAPTER TWENTY-FIVE

Somewhere in the blackness, the infant was screaming again. Cold fluorescent lights fluttered into life overhead, strobing too quickly to actually illuminate the dark. Matt felt himself wandering through the flickering shadows of the crèche barn, searching for the screaming child. Splatters of red marked the straw-lined floor. There were more splashes of blood up ahead. Matt followed the trail, dreading what it would lead to, but compelled to follow anyway. The screaming grew louder as he approached a bedding area piled thick with mounds of wet straw. Matt leaned in over the blood-soaked clumps of stalks to see what was on the other side.

It was a baby.

Almost.

The screaming, twisted infant was a miniature Henry, but even more disfigured than the adult version. Matt took a step back in disgust. As he did, he noticed another figure standing next to him. The other man was dressed in Calham's blood-stained overalls, holding a gleaming scalpel in his hand.

Matt turned to look at the other man's face.

It wasn't Calham.

It was him.

The *other* Matt stared back at him with heavy, dark eyes set in ashen, gray features. Matt thought this double looked dead to him, despite the fact that he was on his feet.

"It's time," said the *other* Matt.

The *other* Matt quickly raised the scalpel and lashed out, whipping it across Matt's face.

* * *

Calham awoke from the dream with a start and sat bolt upright in bed with panic in his eyes. He stared at the collage of victim photos adorning his bedroom wall and let out a deep breath, as familiarity bled through to his waking mind.

He was Calham.

He was Calham, not Matt.

He was the master, not the servant, the slaughterman, not the pig.

The feverish intensity in his face relaxed a little. Calham wiped away the sheen of sweat covering it with the bed sheets and then noticed the sun streaming in through his window. Calham stared out through the glass at the fierce sun, now high in a clear blue sky. His features darkened with worry, and he snatched his watch off the bedside table to look at it. His face fell when he saw how late it was.

"Oh no..."

CHAPTER TWENTY-SIX

Calham quietly approached Matt as he slept, hanging by his arms from one the barn's support beams like a side of beef. He silently released Matt from his chains and let him slide out of them and slump to the floor. Matt crumpled against the straw-strewn floorboards and stayed there.

He was done.

The farmer stood over him for a moment, watching him, thinking. Calham knew this was probably his last moment to reflect on the nature of their strange relationship, before events would almost certainly accelerate them into their inescapable, violent conclusion. He'd wanted more from this, but it was not to be. Years of working against and then with nature had taught him not to fight fate. Things happened, things changed, and you had to roll with the punches. You planted crops and sometimes they grew and flourished, and sometimes they withered and failed. Feast or famine, you had to accept what you couldn't command and move on. No, if this was not to be, then so be it. Move on, lets the seasons turn.

Matt felt the weight of Calham's sombre stare when he looked up, and he sensed something different about the farmer. He stared at the older man's tired, lined features and graying eyes, and saw a look he knew well; maybe he was done with the game too.

"Let's finish this," said Calham.

Matt stood up and fixed his old adversary with a look of defiant contempt.

* * *

The two men marched up the slope and out across the fields at a brisk pace, despite the oppressive heat from the midday sun. Matt stumbled over the uneven ground, dragging the shovel through the earth, as they headed towards the fallow field. His face was bruised and gashed, his leg and hand stained with dried blood from his injuries the night before. Though Matt wavered and swayed as he tried to maintain a straight line, physically and emotionally drained by his ordeals, Calham maintained a cautious distance and covered him with the shotgun as he brought up the rear. The farmer carried a large roll of tarpaulin tucked under his arm. Matt looked at it and wondered what it was for. He heard the rise of a familiar sound as they crossed into the fallow field and continued walking: the low, incessant hum of unseen energy spilling from the earth there. Calham rubbed his aching temples, feeling the effects of the night before, and a growing dread of what he might find upon unearthing Henry after such a long a spell in the field.

They made their way out into the centre of the fallow field.

"Wait," said Calham.

Matt halted and turned around to face the farmer. Calham scanned the field with a worried look on his face. He was trying to remember where they had buried Henry in the early hours. In the excitement of the previous night, he'd forgotten to leave the shovel as a marker. Calham rotated through three hundred and sixty degrees looking for the grave, only to end up facing Matt again with no clue as to the whereabouts of the creature. He looked at Matt pleadingly. Matt smirked at him darkly and shrugged his shoulders. The farmer lit a cigarette and took a long drag, hoping it might help him think. He looked at Matt again and then nodded at him to carry on walking. Matt moved off, but deliberately dragged his feet. He moved lazily, enjoying watching Calham squirm, as he searched the field in confusion. Matt slowed in the haze of the noon day sun and eventually stopped, no longer caring. He began sniggering to himself. Calham turned to look at him with dark, tired eyes, his anxiousness at having lost Henry now obvious. He frowned at Matt and gestured with the shotgun for him to keep on walking. Matt just smiled and gently shook his head. Calham drew closer and pointed the shotgun directly at him.

"You keep pointing that pop gun at me," said Matt. "And it's lost its effect."

Calham advanced, pushing the muzzle towards Matt's face.

"Move," he said.

Matt remained calm and resolute.

"No," he said. "I'm not playing anymore."

"I don't have time for this," said Calham. "He's been in the ground too long."

"Henry?" said Matt. "That thing was overripe the first time you dug it up."

Calham started to speak, then hesitated.

"He's my son," he said finally.

Matt's face creased in a moment of confusion.

"That thing was your son?" he said. "And you brought him back?"

Calham said nothing, but his silence and guilty eyes spoke volumes.

"You've got to help me find him," he said.

Matt stared straight back at the farmer and slowly shook his head again.

He really was enjoying this.

Calham took a step forwards, aiming the shotgun at Matt's head.

"Help me," said Calham.

It was still an order, not a plea.

Matt shook his head again, keeping his eyes fixed on the farmer. Calham thumbed back the hammer on the shotgun.

"You're going to do me anyway," said Matt. "Here's as good a place as any."

The two men's eyes bored into one and other, and revealed that neither was willing to back down. It amused Matt to think that his compliance was still more important to this madman than actually saving his twisted son's life. But then life and death weren't what they used to be.

Finally Calham snorted and lowered the shotgun. He dropped his stony poker face too and began to blink, again looking just as exhausted as Matt.

"Fair enough," he said. "End of the road for us all then."

Calham cradled the weapon in the crook of his arm and began to unroll the tarpaulin. Matt watched him step back, put the shotgun down and snap the tarpaulin out open. The farmer then let it float down over the strange ground to cover it. He then backed up and raised the shotgun again.

"Stand on it," he said.

Matt stared back at him, finally realising what the sheet was for. He stayed still, refusing to step on it.

Calham digested this and grinned at Matt, enjoying the restoration of their power balance and his ability to still inspire fear in others. He nodded and continued to grin, happy to be playing their game again one last time. He began to slowly circle Matt, so as to face him from the other side of the field, forcing Matt to turn with him to meet his stare. The result was that the younger man found himself with his back against the tarpaulin sheet anyway, so that it would be there, ready to catch his blasted remains when the farmer fired. Calham raised the shotgun again, a look of ugly delight spreading across his weathered face.

"Wouldn't want to get any of me on your precious field, would we?" said Matt. "Something might grow. Come back for you in the middle of the night."

Calham's index finger hovered against the shotgun's trigger, and then slowly began to squeeze.

Matt stared back defiantly, bracing himself for the inevitable. Sweat trickled down the side of the farmer's face and he swallowed, drawing his pleasure out, savouring the moment. The muzzle of the shotgun began to shake with effort, as he held it out and prolonged Matt's agony. Calham blinked away small rivulets of sweat from his eyes and tried to steady his grip on the weapon.

A whimpering sound.

Calham glanced to his right, out of the corner of his eye. Matt was compelled to look as well.

The sound came again.

Calham lowered the shotgun and turned away from Matt to look, as something to his rear broke the surface of the soil twenty feet away. Matt watched this breach with a strange fascination, all too aware that this was the source of the whimpering sound. Even though he no longer cared if he lived or died, he realised he did want to see what this thing would look like after turning and spoiling a second time in the field. What fickle, sickly voyeurs we all were, he wondered.

Long, disjointed fingers pushed themselves free from the earth and clawed at the surrounding soil, as their animal owner reenacted echoes of its previous birth. Calham and Matt slowly converged on the burial site in mutual wonder and horror, as Henry's slick, wet hand emerged from the ground.

Calham dropped the shotgun and drew closer. He fell to his knees and began digging in the earth around Henry with his hands. Matt watched the farmer uncover Henry's slimy and grotesque foetus-like features. The dazed creature wearily tried to raise its huge, heavily veined head, but it seemed unable to support the excessive weight there. Calham worked rapidly, consumed by the job in hand, unearthing Henry's shoulders and chest, then its whole upper torso, revealing a fully-grown figure, despite it being slick with a coating of embryonic fluid. This moist, pale, new incarnation of Henry was similar to the old one in every way but its face. The creature's already awful features had been twisted even further by another failed lifecycle in the field. One bulbous eye was now much larger and higher than the other, and Henry's mouth meandered up and along its sliding features like a runaway zip. The whole impression was one of a melted foetus face slipping away from its skull, as if it was trying to escape its own head.

Calham took hold of the drowsy creature by its sticky shoulders and shook it, as it faltered in its escape from the earth. It was like watching the farmer pull a sickly newborn animal from the belly of one of his livestock.

"Come on, Henry," he said. "That a boy..."

The punch-drunk beast raised its head to try and look at him with odd, blinking eyes. It managed to focus and stopped, recognizing the voice and the blurred features before it. Its wild and uneven mouth slowly opened to reveal clusters of jagged tooth shards, as it tried and failed to speak to its father. Only groans and wet whimpers managed to escape its hideous mouth as it dribbled, then the creature's enormous head lolled back down again under its own excessive weight.

"Come on, son," said Calham. "You can do it...'

Calham slapped the beast's face, trying to rouse some fight in it, trying to force life back into something that had already died long ago.

Matt looked on in disgust. Then his eyes moved to the discarded shotgun.

Calham began to shout at the creature called Henry, as its faltered and the strangled, knotted organs inside began to fail and shut down.

"Come on!"

"Let it die," said Matt.

Calham struck Henry harder and harder with his open hand.

"Live!" he shouted.

"Look at it," said Matt. "It wants to die."

Calham spun around and snarled at Matt.

"Look, you fuck..." he began.

But he stopped dead when he saw Matt holding the shotgun, and that it was pointed at him for a change.

A smile slowly spread across the insane farmer's face, and he started to chuckle to himself. Calham's laugh grew louder and more hysterical, as he shook his head, unaware of a low growling sound slowly rising behind him; unaware that Henry was slowly rising too, raising its awful, angry head towards him. Matt's eyes grew wide, and he instinctively took a step back out of Henry's range. Calham's laughter died out, as he caught the look of fear on Matt's face. The farmer slowly turned to see Henry's rabid, dribbling mouth opening behind him. The farmer's lips parted to say something, but the creature lunged at him from its grave before he could speak.

Matt retreated further, as father and son clashed, violently thrashing and writhing in the fallow soil. Blows were struck on both sides, and the two killers locked arms, each trying to gain the upper hand. Then Calham broke off from the contest. Metal glinted in the sun as the farmer quickly raised something into the air and then repeatedly thumped it down into the creature's bloated head, making it squeal. Calham stabbed Henry three times, then scrabbled to his feet and stood over the creature's twitching body, his knife poised for another attack. Henry bobbed about drowsily for a moment, then let out a last wheezing gasp from its mangled mouth and slumped back into the soil. Blood leaked out from its punctured head and soaked back into the fallow field. Calham watched the creature spasm and twitch, as it rode out its shuddering death throes. Eventually they subsided, and the thing that had once been his son was quiet and still.

"He was going to kill me," said Calham. "My own flesh and blood."

"Takes after his father," said Matt.

The farmer looked up from his self-obsessed daze. He turned to face Matt, wiping Henry's blood from his ruddy, red face. He looked carefully at the shotgun, now leveled at his chest.

"Oh you," said Calham. "Where were we?"

"You were about to kill me," said Matt. "Again."

Calham rose and smiled at Matt, before casually approaching him. Matt saw a blade hidden in the farmer's hand glint as it caught the sun. He braced himself against the shotgun's stock and leaned into it, aiming the weapon at the older man.

Calham stopped in his tracks.

Busted.

He forced a smile.

"Funny thing about us," he said. "I kept bringing you back, time after time. Must have got quite attached."

"Yeah?" said Matt.

"When it came to the crunch, back then, just before Henry, I couldn't do it. I couldn't shoot you."

Matt raised his chin and waited to hear what else the farmer had to say for himself.

"I couldn't shoot you," said Calham. "I couldn't shoot you, but I just killed my own son..."

Matt tightened his grip on the shotgun.

"...and last night I saw you, standing over me, with a blade. You could've gutted me in my bed, but you didn't, did you?"

Calham took a step closer.

"You couldn't kill me," he said. "Any more than I could kill you."

Another step.

Matt thumbed back both hammers on the shotgun. Rob's dead face stared back at him from the recesses of his mind. That was the one sight he would never, ever forget, no matter what happened to him.

"A lot's happened since then," he said.

Calham's conniving eyes searched Matt's face for signs of forgiveness or weakness.

He found none.

Realising that his time was in fact finally up, Calham found himself gazing down at the strange soil that had inexplicably resurrected so many of his victims. There was genuine look of wonder in his eyes for a moment, and he began to ponder its unexplored possibilities; possibilities way beyond his own needs and games; but then the look was gone again. He stared at his final victim with something like acceptance and slowly nodded.

"Right," he said. "So, I suppose the next question is, what are you going to do once you've pulled the trigger?"

Calham began to slowly approach Matt again, knowing full well what this would mean.

"Are you going to put me in the ground here?" he said. "Bring me back?"

Matt tightened his grip on the weapon, as the bloodied farmer drew nearer.

"Maybe out of curiosity?" said Calham. "Maybe out of the guilt you'll feel after you've killed me?"

Calham now stood directly in front of Matt.

Close enough to spit on.

"Or maybe you'll want to bring me back..." said Calham. "...just so you can kill me again."

Matt's eyes focused on the neighbouring cornfield in the distance behind Calham. The field where Rob's broken body lay buried without any hope of return.

"Who knows," said Calham. "Maybe you'll get the taste for it after all..."

This last insult was too much for Matt. The thought that Calham still felt, deep down, that they were the same was too much for him to bear.

He squeezed the trigger and watched Calham's midsection disintegrate into a fine red spray. The farmer split in two, his severed upper body spinning up, tumbling through the air, as his legs wobbled and collapsed to the ground. The farmer's upper body finally landed in the earth some feet away from the rest of him with an unceremonious thump.

Matt slowly lowered the shotgun and stared at what was left of the farmer's remains, scattered over his own field. Matt's features were cold, his eyes held no remorse. In that moment he felt absolutely nothing. He dropped the shotgun and knelt down in the field, instinctively digging his fingers down into the earth. He looked out across the fallow field and Shadowbrook Farm, and into the deserted green landscape that lay beyond. He rubbed the strange soil between his fingers and studied it for a moment. He then looked again at the dead farmer.

Dark, unwanted thoughts began to invade his mind.

He began to wonder.

CHAPTER TWENTY-SEVEN

The wall of Calham's bedroom was still adorned with an even spread of Polaroid photographs showing those both unfortunate and fortunate enough to have been resurrected by the fallow field.

But now there were no gaps.

It was completely covered.

The last row of photographs there had been rearranged and re-stuck to the wall's surface, showing a successive parade of confused victims blinking at the camera's flash. Each of the pictures had been snapped in the crèche barn, showing the various victims still tethered there in the straw-strewn bedding area. Matt could be seen again and again amongst the blinking victims on the last row of photos, looking equally dazed from his own repeated resurrections. There was a photograph of the woman taken at the bend in the road too, from the time Matt was forced to witness her abduction and slaughter.

Then there were the pictures of Calham.

These showed the farmer bound in the bedding area too, looking just as lost and confused as the other children of the fallow field. There were more than a dozen photographs of Calham showing his various resurrections.

Like Matt, it appeared the farmer had now died and lived many times over.

* * *

Something stirred in the blackness.

The sound of a heavy door slowly creaking open and slamming shut was followed by steady footfalls, heavy, but soft, and drawing nearer. Someone close by was breathing fast and shallow, as their heart began to race.

A sackcloth hood was yanked up and off Calham's face, making him squint against the glare of the barn's fluorescent lights. He blinked repeatedly as his eyes slowly grew accustomed to the light. He caught sight of something being raised in front of him, but his vision was still blurred. A sudden, blinding flash made him recoil and screw his eyes shut again. Calham moaned pathetically, before opening his stinging eyes again. Another blurred image moved towards him.

He flinched.

Then the image slowly slid into focus.

A masked figure stood in front of him, cocking his head to one side, staring at Calham with a sense of lazy fascination. The man was dressed in dirty overalls and wore a black ski mask. There was a gleaming scalpel in the man's hand. It caught the light as he played with it. Calham's eyes fixed on the scalpel and began to swell with fear. The figure slowly pulled off his black ski mask and stared at Calham with a cold, emotionless lack of expression.

"Hello again," said Matt.

Calham's own expression became one of utter terror. Though his inherited memories weren't yet clear, somewhere in the back of his mind, he instinctively remembered pain from his past lives. A lot of pain. Pain associated with the man now standing in front of him.

And Calham was once again afraid.

THE END

Printed in Great Britain
by Amazon